A SLIGHTLY ABSURD TALE

John Woods-Meakin

 **New Generation Publishing**

A SLIGHTLY ABSURD TALE

Author's Note

The background used in this tale is true. Beirut *did* experience a civil war and the reconstruction of Beirut Central District *is* being overseen by Solidere. The St George Hotel exists, but at the time of writing it is an empty, war-torn shell of a building in Minet el Hosn, Beirut, and its owner is not the person named in the following pages. In this tale of adventure, although existing place names and company names figure, the events described are entirely imaginary.

All the characters in this book have no existence outside the imagination of the author, and they have no relation to anyone bearing the same name or names. They are not even distantly inspired by any individual known or unknown to the author other than liberal use of the author's and his wife's names as principal characters.

John Woods-Meakin
Beirut
May 2003

Thank you for humouring me my darling Felicity

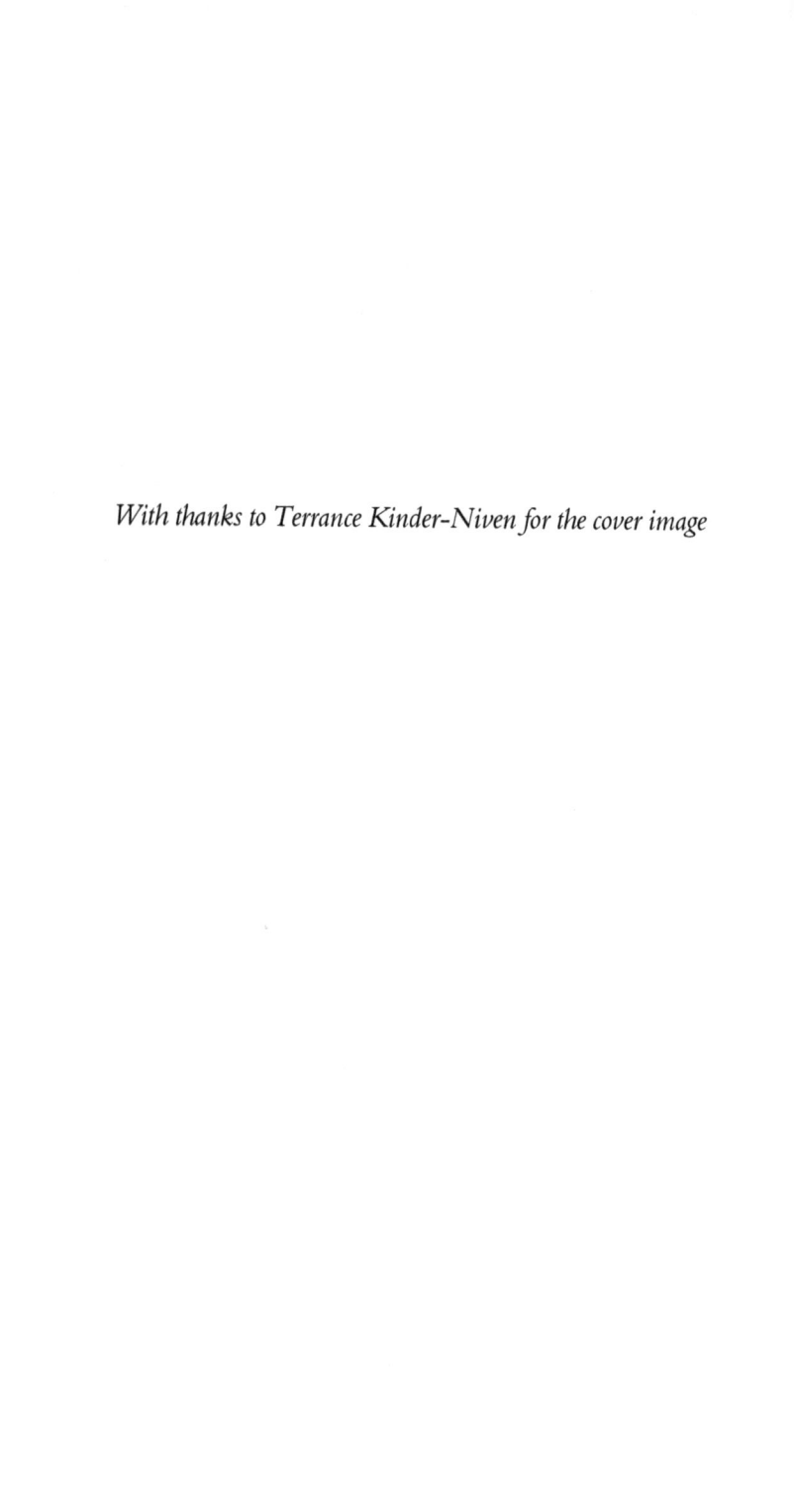

With thanks to Terrance Kinder-Niven for the cover image

Chapter 1

Samantha rubbed her nose. It was small and sculptured. It peeked out from an oval face which was crowned with a bubble of unruly blond hair. Oh, why can't I be like other women – or even a man! she thought, as she contemplated a sleek couple striding towards the cloakroom. Why did God, or rather my mother, have such a lavatory brush – and why did I have to inherit her genes and not Dad's? Dad has such nice straight dark hair, full of body and sex appeal. She suddenly thought of the last time she had seen her father. '…Gee but Dad's bald now…' She considered middle age as a bald woman. It would be different, she thought gleefully, as she imagined herself in a variety of wigs, tailor-made to suit the various social occasions. Perhaps Mum's genes are not so bad; at least it's permanent. She remembered her diminutive mother, her tiny feet and the uncontrollable mass of red hair festooned all over her face; her mother's crooked mouth, caused by constant blowing back of the hair so she could see where she was going and what she was eating. Laughter lines were already etched into Samantha's face, and when she smiled the sun shone through her eyes.

Her father was an adventurer by inclination and an architect by profession who had forsaken the conventional route of bringing up a family.

Samantha had been born in Dubai, and had lived in at least five countries before her prep school days. He still writes as if I should remember these countries, she mused. I was only four-and-a-half when we all came home to Ayot for our education. Dad would often arrive at the house, dishevelled from his long flight to Heathrow; his deep voice commanding attention as he thrust presents in the general direction of his wide-eyed children, trying, as he did so, to negotiate the general direction around rolls of drawings and his beloved T-square. But it was the smell that always announced his return. A sort of manly odour intermingled with Arabian spices and garlic. Mum would always say to him when he returned after one of his trips, 'Darling, when did you last shower?' with the sort of exasperation that is associated with constant repetition. The trouble with Mum was that you could never be certain which way she was facing unless you looked at her feet. The response was generally the same, some sort of grunt, a resounding kiss into that forest of hair covering Mum's face, although it was invariably to the back of the head, before he was off to his beloved office.

Samantha's thoughts were interrupted by the sudden presence of a tall, very handsome young man. Simon had inherited his father's physique and his mother's temperament. Brother and sister greeted each other with affection, Simon taking Samantha's arm and leading her to the nearest cafeteria for an early morning cup of lukewarm coffee.

Heathrow had been quiet during Samantha's wait, but early morning flights were now disembarking passengers arriving at London Airport, heaving with excitement at the prospect of the delights that London had to offer. The occasional businessman with a stony expression, like a full stop in a sentence, regularly interrupted the troop of smiling faces appearing out of the arrivals gate. Simon placed two cups of coffee on the table and sat down beside Samantha. His expression was sober, his eyes alive and sparkling. Of all the men that I know, thought Samantha, Simon must be the best looking. As if to confirm her thoughts, young air hostesses, passing on their way to their respective destinations, glanced at the table where Simon and Samantha were sitting. For some the thought of '*if only*' momentarily blanked out the mental list of the multitude of chores that they must attend to before take-off.

Simon whispered to Samantha, 'Did you receive Dad's last letter?'

Their father had returned to Beirut some fourteen months ago. Their mother had followed separately, although on her arrival at Beirut International Airport, there had apparently been some trouble with her passport. Something to do with her passport photograph.

'It's a bit mysterious,' replied Samantha.

As Simon looked at his sister he saw, momentarily, a flash of concern. Simon had qualified as a lawyer and was practising International Law with one of the large London firms. He would generally joke that being called to the bar was all about extending licensing hours, but Samantha knew about his habit of often working until dawn if he felt his clients' interests were at stake. He looked fit and well as he sipped his cup of coffee.

'I'm worried,' he whispered to Samantha. 'There's much at risk here. What does the old man think he's doing?' One of the passing air stewards, a young man in his early thirties, winked as his eyes locked with Simon's. Struggling to contain his amusement, Simon whispered, 'We've got to go out there.'

Samantha realised the urgency of their parents' predicament, but was suddenly afraid of the prospect of drinking the now cold coffee. 'Please can we have some hot coffee, Simon, this stuff is awful.' It would give her time to think and phrase her response to her brother's decision.

They had lived in Beirut in the early seventies and were forced to leave due to the escalation of violence. Dad had said that he didn't mind being shot at, but he took great exception to his wife and children being exposed to the atmosphere of fear that was beginning to permeate the place. Samantha recollected Beirut in those early years: Mrs Abaid's playgroup, the wonderful people and the sunshine. She remembered the sunshine most of all. What went wrong? she wondered. Why did all those people have to suffer and for what? Both she and Simon had visited Beirut since their parents had returned to the place they had loved more than England. She pictured the empty eye sockets of the burnt out buildings, the devastation and squalor around the ruins of Beirut. Family friends made in those early years were dead, but the spirit of the people remained unconquered and their hospitality and laughter were the same. How could they have lived through all that horror and have survived emotionally unscathed? She remembered the headmaster of the local school in the village where her parents were living. His school had been destroyed, his wife killed, his children scattered, and yet he insisted that he must be allowed to treat them to a real Lebanese dinner at one of the best mountain restaurants. What an evening they had had! On her return to London, she had immediately visited her gymnasium but it had taken over three months to loose the extra weight gained during her holiday.

The crash of breaking china broke her thoughts. Simon had waved to one of the passing air hostesses with whom he was acquainted and three of them had waved back. He had dropped the plastic tray, breaking the cups in his embarrassment. 'Damn,' he muttered, 'sorry about that. This breakfast meeting is becoming expensive. I'll go and fetch some more coffee.'

The cafeteria was filling up fast with an international crowd. Some were biding their time until their flight was announced; some had completed the first exhausting leg of their journey and had decided to explore Great Britain, or as much as was available within the precincts of Heathrow International Airport; others were just waiting to meet arrivals. The wait for hot coffee was longer this time and Samantha was becoming impatient. Simon, breathing heavily, slid into the chair next to her.

'Sorry I was so long. Some bloody man thought that black coffee was an insult to his race and he had a fearful row with that fat woman over in the corner. Everyone just watched.'

Samantha sipped her coffee in silence, wondering how she could respond to Simon. The row in the corner had intensified and the big fat woman was being assaulted by the most extraordinary person Samantha had ever seen. He was as thin as a rake with enormous feet and hands and a tiny head. Perched on his head was a top hat which, in conjunction with his high-heeled boots, gave him stature that his little body belied. Wrapped around the base of the top hat was the most enormous illuminated bow tie.

'Simon,' Samantha said, 'are you being serious about us going to Beirut and, if we do decide to go, what can we achieve?'

'I don't know,' muttered Simon, 'but we won't achieve much by staying in the UK.'

'I can't just walk out of my job – nor can you,' Samantha sighed, conscious of her commitments to her flatmates and to that nice Mr Jones, her boss.

The row in the corner had reached a crescendo. The little man was on the floor, his top hat still firmly in place, but all that could be seen was the illuminated bow tie flashing intermittently as the fat woman, toppling over, smothered him in the folds of her flesh.

'Simon,' said Samantha, have you seen Pierro recently?'

'Why?' replied Simon.

'Well, you know that he and Franco had that awful row about Pierro's Porsche, and you know that Franco had some strange friends. Well, Dad told me once that if we ever needed help, to go and see Pierro and Franco.'

'They are not on speaking terms, so how can they help?' Simon muttered.

'I don't know, I'm just repeating what Dad said. Let's get out of this place. I must go up to London. We can talk in the car.'

Simon had flown down that morning on the early shuttle from Birmingham. He had telephoned Samantha the previous night to ask if she would meet him at the airport as there was something urgent that they must discuss. Samantha thought, '…Ah, he wants a lift to the office…' They both worked in the West End. Samantha was with an international recruitment agency where she was PA to the Managing Director. The traffic on the M4 was heavy as early morning commuters arrowed their way into the metropolis. Samantha drove skilfully through the traffic and in silence. Simon, deep in thought about his latest conquest in Birmingham, wondered what her husband would do if he ever found out that his new wife had not visited her sister the previous night. '…Oh, what did it matter…' he thought, '…Mum and Dad are in big trouble; we must find some way we can help…'

Samantha broke the silence. 'Do you remember Dad's first letter immediately after he arrived in Beirut?'

'Yes,' replied Simon, 'it had me in hysterics. The Hoover washing machine placed centrally in the middle of the road to protect an open manhole. Dad thought it was in working order and that it had been placed over the sewer so that it could discharge water directly into the mains. Can you imagine some Lebanese woman washing her clothes in the middle of the M4…! It couldn't happen here.'

'No, not that,' Samantha interrupted smartly. 'It's what he said about the Lebanese being so innovative.'

'What are you driving at?' asked Simon.

'Well, you know. He said it's not what you see that's important, it's what's intended but not obvious.'

'I still don't understand what you are trying to say,' replied Simon.

'What I'm trying to say,' Samantha calmly replied, 'is that although you believe that Mum and Dad are in trouble, what sort of trouble do you believe they are in?'

Simon considered his reply carefully. 'As you know the civil war went on for eighteen years. The various warlords had to fund the fighting and they adopted some unconventional ways of raising money. There was so much counterfeit around that they wouldn't accept paper money. The banks were not trustworthy so they didn't use them, but traded in gold bullion. I believe that Dad has stumbled on a gold bullion cachet on one of his projects.'

The last letter they had received from their father had clearly been written in haste. His writing was always difficult to decipher. Dad had always wanted to be a doctor but his mild dyslexia had precluded him entering that profession. However, he exhibited some of those traits commonly found in the medical profession. Some of his letters had taken hours to read. The last letter had taken longer.

'Why do you think that?' asked Samantha, as she recalled her father's insistence that neither she nor Simon should talk to anyone about his latest project. He was engaged in the refurbishment of one of the old buildings in downtown Beirut. The Lebanese Government had approved the creation of a quasi-private development company to redevelop the old commercial centre, creaming off profits to line their own pockets. The building which their father was currently working on was located in the original Gold Soukh area. He had been terribly excited about the roof structure of this particular building, referring to 'exceptional dragon plates and tie bars.' Appended to the letter had been a schedule of family assets, with clear, precise instructions as to how Samantha and Simon should proceed in the event of their parents demise. It was unusual for their father to be so specific and insistent about secrecy, as his general inclination was to talk to anybody and everybody about all and everything.

As they proceeded up the Bayswater Road, the grandiosity of Marble Arch loomed in front, a monument to the permanency of history as it cast its illusion of solidity and dependability on the melee of passing traffic. Samantha slowed the car to allow a flock of tourists to cross into Hyde Park engaging, as they did so, in animated conversation demonstrated by the waving of arms and silent chattering. She stared at the ancient monument. Its massive bulk stared back without comprehension as to Samantha's predicament. The road was clear as Samantha nosed the car forward, encouraged by more rapidly moving vehicles on either side.

Simon nudged her. 'Can you drop me outside the St James's Club? We'll talk more tonight. I've got this meeting with Sheikh Mohammed first thing. Poor old bugger's got problems with his apartment in Knightsbridge. Can you believe it, during the renovations, one of the workmen found his secret store of liquor! On Wednesday, the cleaner found his corpse in the maid's bathroom, head down in the WC, the floor covered with half-empty Black Label whisky bottles and festooned with Playboy magazines. The blighter had drowned himself in the loo. Can you imagine the embarrassment to the Sheikh? We have to orchestrate a cover-up.'

After dropping Simon off, Samantha drove up the one-way system into Nightingale Square, negotiated the left-hand turn into West Street and then turned into North Street, parking outside No 10, the offices of Regent International Recruitment Agency. The time was 9.05 a.m. Her mind was calm as she subconsciously absorbed the discipline that the familiar six-storey stucco fronted terraced building exuded.

★

Simon contemplated his loose button as Sheikh Mohammed haltingly explained the repercussions of his cleaner's discovery that previous Wednesday. The Sheikh was the Saudi Government's representative to the International Monetary Fund. He had apartments in London, Paris and New York. As Simon listened, various solutions presented themselves. Okay, maybe the old boy was entitled to his 'days off', as his efforts to redistribute Saudi wealth to deserving causes has been considerable and successful. It was due to his direct intervention that the water supply scheme in Yemen had been implemented and that the hospital, the largest in the Middle East, was being constructed. The union between North and South Yemen had not resolved the simmering antagonism between the two halves of the now united country, and the unofficial support of the Saudi Government to the Yemeni hill tribes straddling the disputed border between Yemen and Saudi Arabia had inflamed the general political situation in that country. Sheikh Mohammed had done much to help extinguish the flames of passion. Simon looked up at his client with concealed sympathy. 'I understand that your wife's cousin's nephew is doing a PhD at London University.' The old man nodded in agreement.

'Does he have a key to your apartment?' Simon quietly asked.

Sheikh Mohammed replied, 'Of course, but I have issued instructions to my nephew that he must never use the apartment without my approval. He is an honourable member of my family and he would never disregard such an instruction.'

'Does he have a chauffeur called Hammed, and is it not true that Hammed has a reputation for self-indulgence?' questioned Simon.

The old Sheikh smiled to himself. 'Mr Simon, I believe we have discovered an equitable solution to our little problem. I shall arrange that Hammed be transferred to less onerous duties back in Riyadh without delay. I am grateful for your time, and you may rest assured that if I or any member of my family can ever be of service to you, you should not hesitate to contact me personally.'

The intercom on Simon's desk buzzed as Sheikh Mohammed was being ushered out, curtailing any further platitudes between the two men. Simon touched the 'speak' button and his office was filled with the silky voice of Alison, the Senior Partner's personal secretary. 'Oh Simon, so you are back, how nice. Victor wants to see you immediately.'

Victor Walpole was senior partner of the Walpole, Henderson, Abbott, McEwan and Young Partnership (generally known as 'The Whammy Boys'). The name had significance, as Victor Walpole was the epitome of congeniality concealing a razor sharp and ruthless mind. He exercised the art of deference and encouraged his partners and pupils to adopt a similar technique. The effectiveness of which, many clients and competitors would testify to. His weakness was his passion for collecting Jaguar motor cars, and the current favourite was a 1982 Series 3 Daimler Jaguar 4.2, which always appeared to be in the basement car park – evidence of the long hours he worked.

Victor Walpole stood by the sliding sash window with the sunlight illuminating the silhouette of his rather short tubby figure. He turned as Simon entered his office through the open door.

'Ah, young Simon,' Victor breathed. 'One trusts that you have fully recovered from the rigours of your Birmingham visit, where, one understood you displayed stamina and enthusiasm commensurate with the opportunities provided to you. One is impressed.'

Simon hesitated. Victor Walpole's constant reference to himself in the third person had the effect that this was his final delivery of a conversation that he had previously rehearsed with somebody else. Victor Walpole walked to his desk, wheeled out his chair and gingerly lowered his ample bottom onto the dimpled leather seat. His eyes glinted through his half-moon glasses as he regarded the young man facing him.

'Something rather dramatic has cropped up. One knows about your family connection with the Middle East and as this matter has its roots in that region, one wonders if you would be so kind as to examine the background as one would appreciate your opinion. Perhaps one could expect your report within the next twenty-four hours. Please communicate with Alison so that one can arrange a little conference with Ian.'

Simon took the proffered file from his Senior Partner's hand, mumbling, 'Yes, sir,' as he did so. Simon turned on his heel, as the meeting was clearly at an end, and made his way through Victor's outer office where Alison was sorting through a pile of motor magazines highlighting articles on Jaguar cars for her boss's voracious appetite on that subject.

'Simon… oh, you are looking well,' Alison commented as the yellow highlighter slid down another page. Simon stopped. He picked up one of the discarded journals and idly thumbed through it whilst Allison continued, 'Did you know that the Daimler Jaguar 3 Series was manufactured in Cape Town during the years '82-'83 and that part number 657YUT987 is only available at Bob Hope Motors in Sydney Street, and that part number 137PTY453 was manufactured under license in Bombay? It is available at Colin Hart Auto's in Oxford, and that…

Whilst Simon was considering a suitable reply, Ian McEwan's head appeared around the jamb of the door. 'Alison, I heard that last bit. If you telephone Jaguar direct you will find that it's part number 138 not 137 and it was manufactured in Hartlepool during '79–'83. Dick's Motors in Blackfriars have three left and promise immediately delivery.'

A heated discussion ensued between Alison and Ian on part numbers and stockists of Jaguar components. Simon, feeling outclassed, slowly walked out onto the deeply carpeted corridor towards the sanctuary of his own office. On reaching it he closed the door and, seating himself behind his desk, commenced reading the thin file that Victor Walpole had handed to him.

Samantha was having a busy morning. Even during the recession, the Agency had been busy headhunting dissatisfied senior executives, who, feeling vulnerable, had vested interests in confidential discussions with competitors. Often the emerging appointment had been short-term, but both parties had benefited from the arrangement and the Agency had received their generous placement fees. Samantha's bonus had multiplied every year. The economic climate was changing and demand was more focused on quality personnel for long-term appointments. Samantha shoved the pile of files away from her to provide space for her 'elevenses', an enormous jam doughnut. She had this weakness for doughnuts, and Mrs Fagg, the elderly tea lady, always had a freshly baked one labelled for Samantha. Samantha had finished compiling a short list of applicants for the vacancy of Director of Operations at Murhead International. She would discuss the list later with Mr Jones prior to forwarding it to the managing director of that company. One of the candidates had intrigued her. Paul James had been approached by Mr Jones, but initiating the first meeting had been delegated to Samantha.

Paul James was an ex-naval officer, who having retired in his early forties had taken up the reigns of commerce with a detachment that was discouraging but with a vigour which had secured his rapid ascent to boardroom level. Samantha had been impressed by his response to her initial telephone call suggesting a meeting at the Director's Club in the Strand. Although his manner had been cold and distant at first, he had been extremely courteous. Subsequently he had warmed to the conversation, as Samantha clarified the job specification, although he showed little interest in the financial package on offer, and it was clear that it was with a degree of reluctance that he agreed to meet her. Paul James had been orphaned at an early age, as both his parents had been killed in the Second World War. He and his sister had been brought up by an elderly aunt in Purley, Surrey. It was as if Paul resented the circumstances of his childhood and strove at every opportunity to suppress them. During his preparatory school days he had been the captain of Rugby and, later at Epsom College, was captain of the school Rugby, Shooting and Cricket teams, ending his school days as Head Boy prior to entering Oxford, where he obtained a double first in Engineering and Middle Eastern Studies. He had enlisted in the navy where he rapidly rose to the rank of Captain.

Samantha surveyed the mature man as he wandered into the lobby of the Director's Club, stooping at the porter's desk, where he quietly addressed the porter to obtain directions. Samantha knew from his CV that he was in his early fifties. He had the physical appearance of a far younger man. Tall, with broad shoulders tapering to a slender figure, well-dressed in a tweed suit with a knitted tie falling against a blue and white checked shirt. He was fair in complexion and as he approached Samantha, she was conscious of steel blue eyes that gave the impression of a deep penetration whatever his level gaze rested upon. Their meeting had been amicable, although Samantha detected a reluctance to respond directly to her questions. She had occasionally before experienced this hesitancy about matters confidential between employer and employee, which characterised a strong loyalty trait. Paul James was clearly an honourable man who, whilst intrigued and flattered by the unsolicited interest in him, slightly resented the invasion of his privacy.

As she put the short list of candidates in Mr Jones's 'Confidential Urgent Tray' she reconsidered the events early that morning. Why was Simon so concerned? she wondered. It was a fact that whilst their father had always been a prodigious letter writer, with letters on a weekly basis to both her and Simon, his correspondence had abruptly ceased about a month ago. Secretly she was relieved, as it was always such an effort to decipher his handwriting. Her mother, Felicity, who always telephoned her every Sunday afternoon for a 'girls chat', had not abandoned the habit, and last Sunday's conversation had been perfectly normal. Her mother had obtained a teaching position at a local private school in Mansourieh, where she taught English to those students who exhibited trauma caused by the Lebanese civil war. Many had psychological problems, and it was with great patience that the mental barriers were broken down. Felicity, with her educated English accent, was always thrilled when one of her class had mastered the rudiments of the language. Recently they had had a tremendous giggle about one of the Lebanese boys who, on mastering the words 'okay', insisted in ending every Arabic sentence with an English upper-class 'Oh Kayee?' It had become so infectious that soon the whole school was mimicking him with an inflection that only Felicity could have provided.

Samantha had tried that morning to telephone her mother but without success. Communications with Lebanon were generally difficult under any conditions. She had decided, prior to taking

Simon's concern too seriously, that she would talk with her mother – but then why hadn't Simon? The day's events gathered pace and soon all thought of her parents had been repressed by the frenzy of office work. Her telephone rang at 6.05 p.m. It was Simon

'Hi, Sam. I tried the flat but they said you hadn't returned from the office. I guessed you would still be there. Fancy a bite to eat at Pedro's around 7.30?'

Samantha's awareness of time had evaporated around noon and she suddenly realised that she was famished. 'Oh yes, love to. See you there.'

Emile Abu Raad was Lebanese. He had been forced to flee Beirut during the '75-'90 civil war, and after spending various periods in Cyprus and Canada he had eventually settled in London. London offered stability and opportunity. His first few years were difficult, but with the help of his father's sister's nephew, who ran a successful import/export business from Wimbledon, he had saved and borrowed sufficient capital to purchase a long lease on a basement just off Billingsgate, where he had established Pedro's, a restaurant specialising in seafood that was patronised by other Lebanese expatriates and frequented by the young aspiring London set with a sprinkling of tourists. The eighteen-hour days were over for Emile. He had had time to marry a local girl, Sally, and their marriage had been blessed with three fine boys; Ghassan John, the eldest; Nagy David; and the youngest, Sami Peter. Sally and Emile had agonised for days about the names, but Emile's roots and traditions were firmly in Lebanon. Lebanon was his first love and naming his 'boys' would be a constant reminder of his *Habibtih*.

Samantha quickly found a parking place near to Pedro's, and, having walked the 100 metres to the basement entrance, she descended the steps to the restaurant. Emile always found time to greet his customers personally. As Samantha entered, the action of opening the old semi-glazed oak door set off a chain reaction. A bell rang softly, announcing a new customer. Emile, who was in the process of withdrawing the cork from a bottle of wine, gently placed the bottle of Kefraya on the adjacent table, and turned towards the sound. He immediately recognized his new customer as Samantha closed the door behind her. He saw a beautiful young lady, elegantly dressed, head crowned with an uncontrollable bubble of blond curly hair, her large eyes smiling at him as he approached her. Emile had weaknesses, which included, amongst others, beautiful women and waistcoats. He loved embroidered waistcoats. His passion for waistcoats occasionally resulted in his adoption of a particular favourite which he would wear for weeks until Sally, knowing of the imminent visit of the Health and Safety Inspector, would persuade Emile to have it dry-cleaned. The waistcoat he was wearing that night was particularly vivid. It was his favourite. The multicoloured pattern was bespattered with wine stains and food splodges and his approach to Samantha was accompanied by an odour of his trade.

They greeted each other as old friends with Emile lightly kissing Samantha on each cheek. Initially, the kiss had been restricted to one cheek but as their acquaintance had grown, so had the quantity and intensity of kisses. The foyer was dark, illuminated by concealed ceiling spotlights. The floor was clay tiled, the walls white painted plaster festooned with marine artefacts, including genuine fishermen's nets that continued over to form a false ceiling canopy. Anchors, stuffed fish and many framed photographs of the numerous parties that had been held at 'Pedro's' adorned the walls. The ambience was Mediterranean. Passing from the foyer into the main restaurant was always a surprise. The body of the restaurant was illuminated by candlelight with each cluster of candles twinkling as the flames flickered in the draught. The main bar, located at one end of the room, was illuminated by spotlights and Samantha's eyes were always immediately drawn to it. Emile had converted a traditional open-topped fishing boat into a bar counter with a mirrored back bar. Bar stools casually stood ready. To the left of the bar was a small raised dais for a band, and immediately below the dais was a dance floor. The remainder of the room contained small tables and high-backed chairs, each prepared for the evening trade. The foyer decorations exploded into the main restaurant, and although dimly lit provided the intimacy that Emile had sought. The overall effect was magical, and many proposals of marriage had been made in the confines of 'Pedro's', some ruefully regretted the following day.

It was still early and the restaurant was about a third full. During the later hours, each table would be occupied and the place would be throbbing with laughter and animated conversation. Simon had already arrived and was seated at the bar drinking a beer. Samantha threaded her way through the partially occupied tables to join him. Emile longingly watched her swaying hips as she walked away. Simon saw her approach out of the corner of his eye, beckoned to Michael, the bar attendant, and ordered a glass of Perrier as Samantha sat down next to him.

'What news?' Simon asked as Samantha settled herself on the bar stool and accepted the glass of iced Perrier from Michael. She took her first sip before replying.

'Oh, not much. Just another busy day trying to stand still. How's your day been?'

'My day has been full of surprises,' said Simon. 'Something has happened that may influence what we were discussing this morning.'

'What?' responded Samantha.

'I'll tell you over the meal, although you must understand I can't go into detail. Client confidentiality and all that, but I'll give you a brief outline,' said Simon. Their conversation drifted into a mundane catalogue of the day's events until Simon realised that hunger was taking priority over thirst and suggested it was time to eat. Emile flustered around them as they ordered, each disappearing behind an enormous menu, only to reappear when Emile, satisfied that his young fledglings had ordered appropriately, vanished into the kitchen to give muted directions to his volatile chef. They made their way to the table reserved for them, sat down and were immediately attended to by two of Emile's waiters, laying side dishes and nibbles as a prelude to the meal to come. Simon ordered another beer and Samantha, a glass of house wine. Emile never rushed his customers and both Samantha and Simon visibly relaxed in the familiarity of the surroundings as the pressures of the day gradually began to dissolve. Simon contemplated the tablecloth as he recalled the contents of the thin blue file that Victor Walpole had handed to him that morning.

'Sam, what do you know about the effect of the civil war on the professional people in Lebanon?'

'Not much, only what Dad told us and what he described in his letters,' replied Samantha.

Simon looked at his sister as he recounted what he had learnt earlier that day. 'During the civil war, many of the professional classes had left Lebanon, abandoning their properties and had taken up residence in other countries. They had relocated all over the world but generally to the Americas, Canada, Australia, France and England, where with their excellent education and their natural ability for business they had prospered. As you know, Dad's engaged in the reconstruction programme in Beirut, but did you know that the Lebanese Government, with the onset of internal peace, passed a law saying that war-damaged, derelict property unless reclaimed by the owners and renovated within a certain period, would be forfeited by the owners and the title would automatically pass to the Government? One of our clients is a Lebanese who settled in London. His family own the St George Hotel in Beirut. As his parents are dead, he is the legal successor to the title and he is being threatened with dispossession unless he takes possession within the next six months. Victor has intimated that he wants me to help sort out the legalities and it may result in a trip out there.' Simon smiled inwardly at the thought of a trip to Beirut. His father, although past his prime, had not stifled his praises for the Lebanese women whom he always referred to as 'the most beautiful creatures on earth'. His writing always became more erratic when making this reference and most of his letters made some reference to 'the beautiful creatures'.

'Simon,' Samantha asked, 'when did you last speak to Mum?'

He hesitated. 'Well, not for some time now. You know the problems of trying to telephone. Either the line is dead or it's engaged. I don't know how you can have a communication system that is unofficially shared amongst the whole population.'

Their mother had explained that the available telephone lines were insufficient for the whole population to have their own line.

Often, if neighbours needed to make a telephone call, they would tap into any available line. The cables were accessible as they emerged from the sub-station in a spaghetti of exposed wires, threading their way to the subscribers via fruit trees, electricity pylons and even washing lines. The concentration of these cables was so dense that they often provided protection from the sun, and an unofficial call could, more often that not, be taken in greater comfort than that afforded to the subscriber. Samantha had been horrified during her last visit to her parents, when a complete stranger stopped her in the lane outside her parent's apartment to ask how she was enjoying her job and to enquire about Simon's health. Her mother explained later, once she had stopped laughing, that in the village everybody listened into the international calls because they wanted to improve their English pronunciation.

Samantha wondered how hard Simon had tried to make the call. He was clearly enjoying the drama of the situation and the possibility that this whole crisis could be the product of Simon's fertile imagination immediately established itself in her mind. She made her decision.

'Simon,' she pouted, 'I'm not prepared to take your scare-mongering seriously. Are you sure that you are not imagining the whole thing? It seems to me that your scenario is only based on the curtailment of Dad's letters to us and that his last one was peculiar, even by his standards. I intend to speak to Mum as soon as possible and find out what is really happening.'

Simon's expression changed from professional intimacy to childish disappointment.

'...He thinks I'm taking control...' thought Samantha. '...Damn right I am...'

Chapter 2

Felicity adjusted her Alice band for the umpteenth time that night. Collette and Fergal had just departed and prior to retiring to her bed, she thought she would linger a moment on the balcony of the apartment. The apartment was on the fifth floor of a six-storey block located in the village of Mansourieh, eight hundred feet above sea level and fifteen kilometres distant from Beirut. The ground in front of the apartment fell away steeply giving its occupants panoramic views over the whole of Beirut and the Mediterranean. Felicity gazed at the twinkling lights of the once renowned city below and at the seeming mirror image reflected in the black night sky above. She had always had this need for space, and the void between the bustling activity of Beirut beneath her feet and the twinkling Mediterranean night sky satisfied her inner being like no other she had ever experienced. She felt she could remain there forever. She felt the emptiness about her, such depth, such tranquillity and such harmony with nature. She savoured the cool night air sweet with the perfume of pine and her thoughts began to drift.

John had had a difficult evening. Whilst he was particularly fond of Fergal, the young Irish engineer, he found it inexplicable that every time Fergal visited them, they always had electrical supply problems. It was John's bad luck that he was obliged to fiddle in the meter cupboard down in the cellar of the building. He savagely thrust his screwdriver into the mass of cables, cursing as he did so. They have all the fun, he thought, whilst I'm down here playing snakes and ladders with a lethal competitor. Where do all these bloody wires go to? I know the problem is a bad connection – but which one, for God's sake? Last time Fergal and Collette came we went through ten candles and four bottles of Ksara. At least, they did. All I had was a bloody shower ten minutes before Fergal and his wife left. Perhaps they concluded that I don't live with Felicity as we have never had a full dinner together. All they see of me is me in my glad rags, opening the door, cracking the first joke of the evening, then the power goes, and I vanish into the bowels of the earth to reappear with electricity restored ten minutes before they leave.

Nabil had volunteered that evening to look at the electrical supply problem. Nabil lived with his wife and three children on the top floor and he had the responsibility of maintaining the block in the absence of the landlord. Initially, John had greeted the suggestion with relief, having silently given vent to his anger on the unprotected face of the apartment front door prior to reporting the fault to Nabil. It had occurred within five minutes of the appearance of Collette and Fergal. Previous scarring marred the massive cedar timber panel of the carved double door to the apartment. Felicity had quietly objected when Nabil later appeared in the dining room wearing only his Y-front underpants and vest. The shimmering candlelight cast grotesque shadows over his body, emphasising the bulbous concealed shape of his various parts. Conversation ceased as Fergal and Collette stared in amazement.

'Darling,' she whispered through her hair to John, who was halfway through his roast beef, 'do we really have to have another cabaret act tonight? Can't you go and have a quick look. You should know what to look for by now. It will only take a few minutes.'

John surveyed his half eaten dinner. Then he glanced at Fergal, who had recovered his composure and was clearly amused, and stomped out of the room taking Nabil's arm, and thanking him profusely for his ineffective efforts. John violently pulled an unidentified cable from the connection box, pushed the white lever to its 'On' position and reconnected the live cable. 'Thank God,' he breathed as the 'On' switch stayed in place. That's got it, he thought. 'Goody, back to my roast beef.' By the time he had climbed the stairs to the fifth floor – the lift was again non-operational – John was sweating profusely. A quick shower and then I'll join the others, he thought.

Felicity had closed the apartment front door after his departure and unfortunately that evening the doorbell had refused to announce visitors by playing its normal melody of 'Happy

Birthday to You', and John was reduced to hammering on the door to let those know inside that he was outside wanting to come in. The door of the adjacent apartment opened and Mr Harb, their elderly neighbour, peeked through the narrow gap to acquaint himself with what was happening.

John didn't hear the greeting thrown at him by his neighbour. All sound was drowned by the music and laughter emanating from within his own apartment. Night sounds were common around the apartment as many of the aging vehicles, panting their way up the steep hills through the village, bellowed forth a throaty roar as defective exhausts could no longer silently conduct the exhaust gases to their final orifice. The dawn chorus was consequently different to that in England as the vehicles retraced their way down the hills to Beirut. John was losing his patience as his tempo of hammering on the sturdy cedar panel increased. Finally he heard somebody from inside his apartment say, 'Isn't the wind strong tonight. It's rattling your front door like crazy.'

Mr Harb offered immediate relief and John turned in disgust and approached the old man. 'What about an arack, old chap?'

Mr Harb nodded, beckoned John into his apartment, and the lift landing between the two apartments at long last fell silent as Mr Harb closed his door behind John's retreating back. John was starting his sixth drink when he thought he heard the sound of voices. Rushing to Mr Harb's door, he threw it open and saw, by the light shining from the inner hall, Fergal and Collette framed in the doorway of his apartment, thanking Felicity for a most enjoyable evening and a super meal, although expressing regret that John had been called away again. 'Perhaps we will see him next time,' he heard Collette say to Felicity. John groaned at the thought of 'next time'. Felicity blew her hair away from her eyes to give herself greater vision and as she did so, caught sight of John's bulk hovering in the adjacent apartment doorway.

'Oh, there you are darling. Oh, where have you been? Didn't you remember that we were having Collette and Fergal to dinner tonight?'

John hurriedly thanked old Mr Harb for his hospitality and approached, not in a direct straight line, the departing couple.

'Gladsh thatsh yoush enjoyedsh yourselvesh. Sorrrry thatsh I wash bussy,' he mumbled, prior to staggering into his apartment, where he headed in the general direction of the bathroom.

★

Sami Hassan scratched his groin as he surveyed, with unconcealed anger, the motley assembly around him. Each member of the assembly eased himself into an obstructed position by concealing himself behind his immediate neighbour. The restrictions within the dimly lit room abruptly terminated this shifting of shadows. Sami' s glare focused on Omar Ouma, his former henchman.

'What do you mean, you can't find it?' The room rocked with the sound of Sami's voice as he gradually became more incensed. 'Do you realise exactly what you are saying, you fool!'

The soft sound of knocking knees provided an intimidating background as Omar, snivelling with self-pity, replied with a voice taut with tension, rising in pitch after each word had been uttered. 'It's not where Ali expected it to be. It's his fault, not mine. He had the responsibility to conceal it. You should question Ali. He's here. Ali, why can't you find it…?' Omar's voice had reached the top of the scale and was no longer audible. Only the ending to his protestations could be heard as a slight hiss.

Sami sat behind a worn wooden desk. His enormous bulk, supported by an old wheel-backed wooden chair whose tenon joints had long ago given up any pretence of being quietly functional, creaked and groaned as the weight above fluctuated with the rise and fall of vented anger. The room was illuminated by a low wattage bulb suspended from the dirty ceiling by a crooked wire. A spider, who minutes before had been silently spinning his web to snare his evening dinner, vanished into the gloom of the tattered cornice. Sami lowered his eyes to the well-thumbed school exercise book open before him and scanned the last page. Colour gradually returned to Omar's face as he realised that other matters were taking priority over his own life. The room was silent save for the slight dribble of urine bouncing off the concrete floor as Sami contemplated their predicament.

During the fifteen years of civil war, Sami Hassan had commanded a local force of Christian militia and it had taken all of his entrepreneurial talents to arm, clothe, feed and maintain this force. He had discovered that God had given him an opportunity to increase his personal wealth. One of his initial successful enterprises had been the organised theft of vehicles from the wealthy areas of Beirut. Owners could reclaim their vehicles, concealed at a secret location in the Bekaa valley, on payment of a large donation to the Christian war effort. The peace settlement had not interfered with this enterprise, which continued to produce regular high earnings. He had endeavoured to keep the scale of this enterprise within reasonable bounds by restricting his demands to that which the owner could afford. He was forced to adopt this code as, during one of the early thefts, the owner had protested that his employees' salaries had been stolen together with his vehicle, and that unless the money was returned to him, he would be unable pay his workers. Sami was so incensed that the owner should regard him as a common criminal that he returned not only the money, intact, but also the vehicle, although apologising that the condition of the Land Rover had slightly deteriorated during the period it was in Sami's possession. Word had spread, and owners were quite relieved when their vehicles were purloined by Sami's organisation.

His power had grown in proportion to his money, and by the end of the war he was second in command in his district. Although far more wealthy than the District Commander, Sami lacked the family connections of his superior. The onset of peace provided other opportunities, and Sami immediately created a construction company. What better way, he thought, to consolidate his money than by rebuilding that which he had helped to destroy? Sami was a contented man as he had acquired many lucrative construction contracts, and with the reconstruction programme accelerating he was expecting many more. This evening's meeting had shattered this complacency.

The war years had been difficult as paper money had had little value and the banks were vulnerable, at best to robbery, at worst to total destruction. Sami had eliminated this problem by amassing an assortment of antiquities looted from damaged buildings which, through middlemen in the Gulf state of Dubai, had resulted in dollar accounts in the majority of international capitals. The war effort required regular financing from local funds, and Sami had arranged the conversion of part of his dollar account, maintained with the Banco Suez in Zurich, into gold sovereigns smuggled into Lebanon through intermediaries every six months. With this internationally recognised currency he had been able to fund his war effort. The last shipment had accompanied a genuine consignment of arms and ammunition. The bullion had been concealed in a special box marked 'ammunition box' and on arrival it had been quickly spirited away and concealed in a safe haven by a select trusted few. That there had been another ceasefire immediately prior to the shipment arriving had, at the time, been considered of little consequence. All previous ceasefires had been negotiated on the basis of maximising the advantages provided by the uneasy cessation of hostilities. Once one of the warring factions had achieved their objectives, fighting had again commenced. The last ceasefire had unbelievably held, and peace quietly took possession of the devastated country. That those select and trusted few (now fewer than before) were unable to locate the bullion was devastating, as with the establishment of peace and normality it was time to make further provisions in the securement of additional lucrative Government reconstruction contracts. Disposal of the sovereigns would be easy. A coin passed here and there amongst the more influential Government officials would eliminate all competition.

Sami studied the last entry in the makeshift ledger book open in front of him. The page had been slightly stained. Merging parts of the blue ink of the flowing Arabic script had run, many years ago, into the small encrusted rust spots splattered haphazardly over the entries. He was unable to decipher all of the last entry as a neat round black-rimmed hole had entered the page exactly where the entry had been written. He read; 'Special shipment 18: 30,000 Gold Sovereigns: arrival 18.02.91: transported with Salim to 'D…r …r…et', 1 metre down, under…carve…'

This evidenced the enthusiasm in the execution of his instructions that old Amin Hakim, the ancient bookkeeper, should be eliminated once his work was done. Anger swelled up again, but he reasoned with himself that further demonstrations to subdue these fools would achieve little. He must cast his mind back to the night of the 18th February and remember any leads that he could follow in the recovery of his treasure. Sami soon became oblivious to the mumbling and mutterings of the frightened assembly in front of him as his memory took possession of him…

The night of the 18th February had been wet, thundery and very dark. The shipment had been landed by fishing boat in the safe port of Junieh and he had personally supervised the unloading. His work gang consisted of four of his closest associates, Bedo Zahredoline, Marwan Sinno, Jihad Usta and Toufic Karkour, and they had worked by the lights of the old Bedford truck and the Toyota pickup. The special cargo had been quickly identified and it had been stowed in the Toyota whilst the men around him laboured to hoist the rest of the shipment into the Bedford. He remembered the drivers, old Salim at the wheel of the Toyota and young Nabil driving the Bedford. It was his wont that he always accompanied the special shipment to its final destination, but that evening an emergency had arisen and for reasons that he could not clearly recall he had been obliged to change his plans at the last moment and return post haste to his headquarters. He had had few qualms that the concealment would proceed, as planned as this was the eighteenth shipment, and at no time previously had they experienced any problems.

The routine was well established. Old Salim had received specific instructions that he was to rendezvous with Ali and Omar at the burnt-out hulk of the previously prestigious St George Hotel. He recollected that Ali and Omar never made the rendezvous due to Omar's wife suddenly going into labour with her tenth child. It had been a difficult labour and regrettably the baby had died. Ali, being deprived of transportation due to Omar's need to get to his wife, managed to steal an unattended vehicle – only to find, on his way down Corniche Masra, that the brakes were not operational. Sami had been obliged to visit him in hospital the following morning. Old Salim had apparently waited for his companions, but with the approaching dawn he had himself deposited the special consignment in a safe place and later that same day confided the location details to old Amin who had faithfully entered them in the book now lying open in front of Sami. Old Salim was dead. His death was unnatural in those days of violence and bloody slaughter: he had died of natural causes.

Sami himself had been unable to verify the place of concealment or to inspect the ledger. It had then passed out of his mind, as he himself had been the target of an assassination attempt rendering him badly wounded. He mulled over the few clues. The fragmented entry in the ledger, Old Salim's favourite haunts around the St George. No whispers had reached his ears that treasure had been discovered and he was quite certain that it was still safe and undetected in one of the many war-damaged buildings in 'downtown Beirut'. He suddenly looked up. The assembly, still shifting and sliding into one another, were, without exception, studying the rough floor like trainee surveyors intent on identifying any structural weakness in the concrete slab upon which they were standing. He stared at Omar, whose cheeks, hollow by genetic inheritance, looked gaunt and sunken.

'Omar,' Sami growled. Omar raised his head in a series of shaking movements. 'I want a complete list of all streets and building names within an area of 500 metres around the St George, and I want it tomorrow. Ali, I want you to see old Salim's family and find out about his favourite haunts and the places he knew well around that area.' Sami had concluded that by matching the two he might be able to identify the general location of the concealment, sufficient for a detailed search of that area. 'Now get out, all of you except Mohammed. You stay behind.'

The room was immediately vacated as if the opening of the external door activated a giant vacuum cleaner with the assembly, like specks of debris, offering token resistance to the force of the suction. Immediately the door had closed behind the last retreating back, Sami beckoned Mohammed to his side and quietly gave him instructions. Mohammed had to continually repeat these until Sami was satisfied that he had fully understood that which was required of him over the next forty-eight hours.

★

Samantha replaced the telephone receiver with a sigh of relief. The conversation with her mother had only taken thirty minutes, and from London she had been able to dial direct. The fact that she had spent almost two hours trying to get through was a constant source of frustration, but the strangers she had chattered to were all delightful and enquiring and pleased that she had come through on the wrong number, as they clearly had an interest in extending the conversation. Her mother's voice eventually came on line and soon they had entered into a robust conversation interspersed with light laughter about recent events and family future plans. However, the intimacy of the conversation was restricted due to the background of the deep breathing of the silent audience, and it was this that prevented Samantha from expressing her real reason for the telephone call. She had been intrigued by her mother's recital of the events of Ashoura, which had apparently taken place sometime previously in the village of Nabatieh. Her mother explained that the roots of the celebration had been imported from Iran and it was the memorial service of the death of the Prophet's grandson, Hussein. She had described the gruesome events whereby the Shiite Moslems attend the central mosque in the village to receive two taps to the forehead with a cut-throat razor. The streets were soon splattered with congealing blood as the celebrations gathered pace, with many of the participants being hidden behind gruesome red masks. It was the end of the ceremony that had astounded Felicity as she was afforded the unusual sight of blood-drenched motorists nonchalantly driving home as if they had done nothing more than spend the morning shopping in Nabatieh' s marketplace. Whilst the conversation had been fairly normal, any reference Samantha made to her father's work had resulted in a quick change in the topic of their conversation. Samantha was not satisfied that all was as it should be, but, without evidence to the contrary, it was only her intuition that nagged away at her.

★

John took the S-bend at high speed, ignoring the manic hooting of passing vehicles, as he angled his 1990s' BMW 735i into the narrow gap between the dilapidated 1950s Austin Westminster and the wheezing 1940s school bus, crammed with wide-eyed youngsters all giggling at some obscene joke privy to themselves. Every morning he followed the same winding lanes, in his descent to Beirut from the mountain village, and every morning he had expectations of a major incident. He had long ago forsaken the delight of savouring the crisp mountain air warmed by the early morning sun due to the need to beat the worst of the traffic. Leaving the apartment at 6. 15 a.m., he would enter the two-way traffic system that effectively split Mansourieh into three longitudinal parts. Considerable care was necessary to negotiate down the one-way system to avoid the upcoming tractors and 'services' which, seeing the opportunity of avoiding the uphill congestion, adopted the less congested downhill route. The previous morning, he had had to take rapid evasive action to avoid a rogue Nissan Patrol, whose owner, having parked it, left the vehicle with the engine running as he quickly visited the village bakery. In his haste he failed to engage 'Park', and the defective handbrake had not prevented the vehicle from running amok. The two-way system merged into a single road at the end of the village and the Nissan Patrol continued its torturous descent down to the coastal plain surrounding Beirut.

During the summer months many families would occupy their mountain residences, moving down to their Beirut residences with the onset of winter. The beginning of the new school year was always a nightmare as fathers ferried their offspring to the various education establishments dotting the countryside. Those who due to circumstances could not partake of the morning run depended on the old school buses. As John pulled into the space between the two descending vehicles, narrowly missing the upcoming 1930's Mercedes school bus by inches, his mind unaccountably recalled Felicity's school outing the previous week. The school had arranged for the pupils to visit Jeita, the cavern of wonders. Five dilapidated school buses had left the Westwood Academy in convoy. Felicity had been in the first vehicle, seated on a wooden plank in the aisle spanning the two front seats, immediately behind the driver. She had found the views of the road surface beneath her feet interesting, spied through the corrosion that formed voids in the floor decking of the old vehicle. The fact that the driver gnawed his fingernails whilst accelerating down the mountain as he overtook all other traffic was disconcerting, and by the time they approached the 'Best' roundabout to enter into the main traffic routes around Beirut, Felicity's eyes were tightly shut.

An article in the *Daily Star* the following day described the chaos caused by five school buses continuously circulating round the roundabout, as a dispute had arisen as to the correct exit route. The drivers, failing to stop, had shouted the directions to each other from their cabs as they circled. The 1950s Austin Westminster in front of John's 1990s BMW slowed as another passing vehicle forced its way into the gap between the Austin and the vehicle in front. The cavalcade of vehicles continued their descent, slowing at frequent intervals to widen the gap between consecutive vehicles to permit the entry of the more impatient drivers into the procession, like carnivorous beasts gobbling up passing morsels. The procession slowly wound its ways down towards the 'Best' roundabout, with a carnival air of tooting horns, gesticulating arms and Arabic music tainting the crisp early morning mountain air.

John was sweating by the time it was his turn to negotiate out into the solid traffic flow choking the 'Best' roundabout. He made the office building by 7.15 a.m., parked his car in the space provided, exchanged pleasantries with the security guards and ascended by lift to his office. With trembling hands he prepared himself a cup of coffee as his blood pressure returned to normal. The unpredictability of the vehicles currently using the Beirut road network to effectively 'brake' created in those drivers, unconditioned to the habits of the Lebanese, anxiety syndromes so acute that prior to embarking on any journey, anti-acid treatment for the stomach was a necessity.

The Lebanese population had not been in any position to renew their personal means of transportation since the mid-'70s, other than a few exceptions, and the average vintage of vehicles in daily use would have excited Lord Montagu of Beaulieu, representing an inexhaustible supply for his collection, although cosmetic surgery would be a prerequisite to any addition.

Manufacturers' brochures of many vehicles were no longer applicable, as dimensioned lengths at time of manufacture had been altered by the constant ramming of front and back with the consequence that functional brake and indicator lights were a feature of other countries. Drivers patiently waiting at major road junctions lived in trepidation of the adjacent vehicles, as it was only on the changing of the traffic lights that the intent of their drivers would become clear, occasionally accompanied by a loud bang or scraping sound as the inside vehicle cut across the path of the outside vehicle, each turning in the opposite direction to the other. The middle vehicle wishing to proceed directly ahead was caught in a pincer movement and stood little chance of avoiding damage to both offside and nearside wings. Some drivers had removed these embellishments completely, to the general satisfaction of the insurance companies, who welcomed lower repair bills. Traffic lights, those few still functioning, were generally unsynchronised, and it was quite remarkable that the majority of drivers still respected the discipline imposed by this invention. It was not unusual to see at major crossroads, pairs of traffic lights changing colour at exactly the same time, thereby permitting the waiting ranks of panting vehicles to forge into the melee of the inevitable logjam.

That morning John had been awakened by the penetrating throbbing of the alarm and, as he turned towards Felicity, her warm sensuous body curled against him. She stirred and mumbled, 'Oh darling, is it morning already?' Not waiting for an answer, she continued, 'Please can I have a cup of tea?'

Felicity's functional level at the beginning of a new day was accelerated by the results of four cups of Harrods' 'Early Morning' tea. Without the exact quantity and strength of this brew, she would function at a low level until midday and then suddenly leap into a far higher level until well after midnight. John knew the benefits of keeping his wife's metabolism as balanced as possible if he was to get any sleep the following night. While the water was boiling, he quickly showered and completed his ablutions, and whilst waiting for the tea to brew, dissolved some 'Eno' tablets in a glass of mineral water, swallowed the mixture and returned to the bedroom with the tray of tea and a slightly clearer head. The throbbing of the alarm still echoed in his brain. He checked that the alarm was off. It was, but the throbbing continued.

He sipped his coffee slowly, savouring the rich aroma of the bittersweet thick black Arabic coffee as he contemplated the day in front of him. It promised to be demanding, but then every day had the same pressures. He had a meeting at 10 a.m. with Ziad Mneimieh, the Managing Director of the large international consultancy group that had head-hunted him from London; lunch at 1 p.m. with Brian Franklin-Smythe, the Senior Architect for the Council for the Redevelopment of Beirut (CDR) and, at 4 p.m., a presentation to Safwan Nizer, the Saudi developer intent on constructing a massive residential complex with retail outlets at a budget that could not reasonably be achieved. In between these meetings he had to prepare a preliminary feasibility study for the new proposed medical centre in Beit Mary for discussion with the project manager the following day.

The throbbing in his head had subsided and his hand steadied as his mind switched into his favourite auto drive as he began to visualise colours and design integrated with his work. Silver, his beautiful secretary, announced her arrival as she sat down in the adjacent office, switched on the computer and yawned. John was immediately distracted from his creative mode as the sound conveyed all those things promised in the in-flight MEA magazine.

He glanced in her direction. Jet-black shoulder-length hair, falling from a high forehead; skin, the colour of peaches and cream; large black eyes that sparkled and danced with amusement under fine arched brows; an aquiline nose of delicate proportions and a mouth that promised bliss. Silver was a beauty endowed with brains and many capabilities, some of which John knew he had not and never would experience. She entered his office, crossed to his desk and smiled with her eyes at his distorted muscular body as he valiantly tried to ignore her by stretching across the top of his massive desk to regain a pencil that had suddenly appeared almost beyond reach. She placed a yellow file on top of the in-tray and breathed, 'Good morning Mr John, how are you today?' Then she swivelled gracefully on her high heels and left John feeling inadequate as she regained the outer sanctuary of her own office.

The yellow file had been requested by John the previous afternoon, as it contained general construction data about a project that he was responsible for in the BCD area. Two weeks previously he had had a site inspection of a derelict building in downtown Beirut near the St George Hotel. The inspection had indicated that whilst the structure was generally sound, the external walls and internal construction was severely damaged due to constant shelling. He had made the recommendation that the building could be renovated as opposed to demolished, and then reconstructed, as it contained many fine features that, with loving care in restoration, would provide maturity to the complex of new modern buildings being constructed around restored old buildings. The Government had decreed that where renovation was possible, it was the preferred option, as with a blend of old and new, 'Down-town Beirut' would provide unique architectural excitement. The following day, Beirut had experienced one of its frequent earthquakes reading 5.6 on the Richter scale. John had decided that he should reinspect the building to determine how it had withstood the tremors. It had terrified the hell out of him as his office, on the tenth floor, had swayed continuously like a giant plumb bob on a massive string. The area of the building was restricted, being patrolled by the tough Lebanese Army. Access was only permitted by special authorisation.

John showed his pass to the soldiers guarding the entrance of the massive building site and was escorted to the building. The soldiers were not permitted inside and security was necessary to prevent the inflow of squatters into the empty buildings and the theft of building materials. John's inspection showed that the main structure had not suffered any damage, notwithstanding that a few of the internal non load-bearing walls had cracked. As he was leaving, he observed a particularly fine carved stone lintel, and as he approached it, his foot struck a slight projection in the floor. He stooped, cleared away the rubble and exposed the corner of a wooden box. Intrigued at his discovery, he decided to investigate more in the knowledge that he would not be disturbed. He had soon unearthed what appeared to be an old ammunition box and, whilst hesitant, he was unable to control his curiosity. He gently levered off the top, the rusty padlock offering token resistance, expecting to find exactly what the box suggested. Nestling in the bottom of the box were small hessian bags, each top tied with a leather thong. He lifted one, grunting with the effort, and as it slammed down on the paved stone floor due to its own weight, he was surprised to hear the chink of coins. The leather thong was difficult to untie as it had swollen with moisture. John produced his Swiss Army knife and slit the side. Out poured a torrent of small coins, spilling into the dark interior of the building like little globules of gold. John's heart stopped beating as he surveyed the pile of gold at his feet. He remained motionless as his mind went into orbit. A sudden noise outside brought him back to earth.

He quickly replaced the bag in the box as he counted the remaining bags in the gloom. Two levels, each level with twenty bags, was his rapid calculation. He placed the lid firmly back in place and snapped the padlock prior to scooping rubble and earth over the spot so that it was indistinguishable from the other floor areas in the dark building. He was escorted out of the area by the waiting soldiers and signed off his inspection visit at the guarded entrance to the massive construction site. He had pocketed a few of the coins for closer inspection at his leisure and in the relative security of his apartment. That evening he had shown Felicity the coins and their discussions had continued late into the night, as he had forgotten that morning to make the requisite number of cups of tea for his beloved wife.

Chapter 3

Victor Walpole's quietly modulated voice dominated the meeting as he summed up those salient matters that had emerged during the meeting with his client, Mr Kamal Bsat, owner of the St George Hotel, Beirut. 'One may reasonably conclude that as a consequence of the Lebanese Government Decree No. 19438, that a derelict property within the curtilage of Ville de Beyrouth must be physically occupied by the rightful owner and also that evidence must be provided to the Council for the Development and Reconstruction that appropriate measures have been implemented to ensure the restoration of the said property by no later than the fifth anniversary of the date of the decree. Failure to comply with the requirements of this legislation within the period defined within the legislation, automatically grants the elected Government, at that time, an entitlement to confiscate the property without compensation, on the condition that written notice of their intent to so do is served on the rightful owner. One trusts that that is a fair appraisal of your situation so far, Mr Bsat.'

Kamal Bsat nodded his head in agreement. Simon's pen had run out of ink and he glanced at Ian McEwan, who was casually still making notes. Victor continued his monologue.

'The deadline for such implementation expires in nine weeks' time and you can then expect to be served with the written notice. Is that correct?' Kamal Bsat affirmed that it was so. 'Notwithstanding your programme, the current economical and political climate in Lebanon still remains fragile to the extent that it precludes any but the most adventurous international investor, and sufficient financial resources have not yet been realised. Is that correct?' Kamal Bsat again gave affirmation. 'One must say one finds that predicament is wholly inequitable but one believes that one can discern a possible avenue that may be suited to the circumstances and may have the effect of delaying the proceedings. One proposes to…'

Kamal Bsat, Victor Walpole's client, had visibly relaxed, his anxiety decreasing as his confidence in Victor Walpole's ability increased. Suddenly, as if by sleight of hand, there popped into his mouth a lighted cigar and he commenced to puff contentedly as he looked at his future anew. Victor paused, cleared his throat with a slight cough, interrupting his fluent summing-up of that morning's discussions.

'One does beg your pardon, Mr Bsat, for this slight interruption. One does find, however, that fumes produced by smouldering vegetable leaves quite distasteful, and one would respectfully request that you kindly extinguish the said article in the nearest appropriate receptacle. One then proposes to adjourn for ten minutes whilst this room is properly ventilated. One will, of course, have no option but to include this slight delay as a billable item on your account. One endeavours to portray one's wishes to all one's clients by the provision of notices clearly stating that this office is a non-smoking area.'

Kamal Bsat regarded his Monte Cristo cigar with horror. He mentally totted up the cost of the delay, added the cost of the fine Cuban brand and suddenly concluded that at $100 per centimetre of smokable length, it was a luxury that not even his clever accountant could justify. His arm moved in the action, developed during his school days at Whitgift, as he bowled the smouldering cigar clean through the open window where it descended towards the busy public thoroughfare five storeys below. The buzzing of the hustle and bustle of the public had been barely audible during the duration of their lengthy discussions. Victor stared at Kamal Bsat with horror. Initially no change in the decibel level of the public buzzing had been discernible, but this gradually changed until there was a distinguishable commotion, swelling in volume with shouting and screaming exacerbated by the distant ringing of a Fire Engine bell as it rapidly approached the vicinity of Victor Walpole's office. Victor Walpole picked up the telephone receiver, punched in a number and whispered, 'Alison, one would be so appreciative if you would be so kind as to find out the cause of the commotion outside.'

As Victor replaced the receiver, he turned to Kamal Bsat and quietly said, 'One must regret the chosen method of the disposal of your offending article.' Simon and Ian remained silent. The telephone rang. Victor picked up the receiver, listened without comment and replaced it in its cradle. He turned to Kamal Bsat. 'One is informed that your article descended the full height of this building and during its period of free fall received sufficient oxygen to ignite the article to the extent that on landing on the brim of a gentleman's bowler hat, it ignited the said bowler hat. At the time the gentleman was studying his losses on the stock market, and was so preoccupied that he failed to notice that the *Financial Times* newspaper he was reading was in flames. It is understood that he was, figuratively speaking, "being burnt in the market", and the physical apparition of flames was, it was thought, a figment of his own imagination. One is led to believe, that the recipient of your generosity, Mr Bsat, may be outside this office at this very moment.'

As if on cue, a general disturbance could be discerned from the general area of the reception on the ground floor, quickly followed by the humming of the elevator motors. The chime of the lift halting at the fifth floor proceeded the dull echo of heavy footsteps as they rapidly approached the boardroom door. This was followed by a loud crash as an unknown force threw open the heavy wooden double doors with such force that they bounced off the skirting mounted door stops and rebounded onto the dishevelled figure framed in the opening. Victor Walpole gave a deep sigh as he threaded his way around the table towards the still bouncing doors, and the motionless figure of a gentleman, sprawled lengthwise in the corridor. The meeting was resumed later that day.

*

Ian McEwan pressed the 'Enter' key on his computer console as he keyed in the Spellcheck programme. He had spent all morning formulating his notes made the previous day during discussions with Kamal Bsat, the owner of the St George Hotel, into minutes of the meeting. He found it difficult to contain his excitement as this brief had all the indications of departing from the norm. Ian was an excellent lawyer but recently he had developed a restlessness that was alien to his placid nature. His entry into the partnership five years previously had fulfilled his ambition, and he had thought at that time that his future progress into old age would be comfortable and rewarding. Victor was a compassionate Senior Partner and the practice was growing rapidly.

Ian had acquired all those material things that mattered to a professional man. He had a lovely wife, Janette, and two fine boys, both excelling at their respective schools. Whether he would be able to afford Charterhouse for the younger of his sons, William, was a problem that vexed him. Alexander was doing well at Hodgesonites, Ian's old house at Charterhouse, but the fees had risen dramatically since his own days there as a boarder. He was Chairman of the local Rotary Club and a passionate, although rather insignificant, cricket player with the Sevenoaks Cricket Club. He had sometimes mused during some of the matches that the job of longstop was not a high profile position and unfortunately his batting average was rather less than could be reasonably expected from a good player. He would join the 'boys' at the local public house most Friday evenings for a few pints, weather permitting, as he strictly observed the drink-drive laws. It would do his reputation no good to be hauled up in front of the local magistrate for a drink-drive offence. The family always had two holidays each year: one in the South of France in the summer, and at Easter it was down to Bournemouth for a week. It was always the same camping site in France and the same three star hotel in Bournemouth as, whilst Ian's income was large by most standards, the school fees were taking a bigger proportion each year. The family lived in a large, detached modern house in a close of similar large, modern houses. The practice provided Ian with a company car, an upmarket Ford, whilst Janette had a nearly new runabout. All the houses in the close had company cars, and the respective wives all had nearly new runabouts. The only distinction was one of colour.

Ian had always enjoyed commuting and was a 'regular' on the 7.15 a.m. from Sevenoaks to Charing Cross, where he would relax in his first class seat to read that mornings *Times*. All his travelling companions in 'his' compartment read *The Times*. Ian always wore the same suit and tie on each separate day of the week, and the suits with tie would rotate throughout the week to be repeated on the same day of the subsequent week. It was immediately after his 45th birthday that Ian awoke one morning with a feeling of lethargy and he realised, looking at himself in the shaving mirror, that he was in a *rut*. He tried to combat this rising sense of restlessness by initially tying his shoelaces together differently. This was subsequently followed over the weeks by more draconian measures as Ian started to wear odd socks and to rotate his ties, unsynchronised, with his suits in his endeavour to bring a little excitement into his daily routine. These oddities had developed further as his daily reading habits began to embrace the *Sun*. Producing this tabloid in the first class compartment on the 7.15 produced from his travelling companions a raising of eyebrows, but no direct comment, as the pinstriped brigade exchanged pleasantries amongst themselves; but any direct reference to Ian's degenerating reading habits, (in their opinion) was beyond the extremities of their travelling relationships. 'Live and let live, old boy,' was the motto of the regulars on the 7.15 to Charing Cross.

Ian checked his notes against the draft minutes of the meeting that he had just completed. It was evident from the discussions the previous day that Kamal Bsat had been unable to conduct proper investigations in support of key criteria incorporated in his business plan. Potential investors had refused to contribute to the reconstruction programme as they doubted Kamal's ability to comply with the financial returns on capital invested as quoted in his prospectus. Only Murhead International had submitted a qualified 'Statement of Interest subject to further *verifiable* information'. Victor had briefly laid out his milestone objectives the previous afternoon, and it had been left to Ian, assisted by Simon, to prepare and implement the Project Implementation Activity Programme within the period allocated. Victor had reasoned that, prior to any reconstruction programme, it was necessary for the owner to have unimpeded access to the property for the purpose of preparing a detailed dilapidation survey. This survey would provide the data on which all future design activities would be based, and eventually it would contribute to establishing the capital cost of reconstruction, together with the period necessary for reconstruction and thereby the payback period. The business plan would then develop from these identified key elements on a supportable basis. The fact that the property had been occupied by the Lebanese Army as a temporary command post precluded meaningful investigations. The surveyors employed by Kamal Bsat had been obliged to spent more time with Army Intelligence sipping Arabic coffee and passing generally favourable commentary on the tactics adopted by respective players in the traditional game of tric-trac (backgammon), played effortlessly and constantly by the bored but playful Intelligence Officers, than in surveying the war-damaged structure.

Representation had to be made to the appropriate Government Ministry to remove this impediment as a precondition to reconstruction. It therefore followed that confiscation would be legally unenforceable according to the Government's own decree. Ian's immediate task was to make representation to the Lebanese Government. He reached for the telephone, placed his called to the Lebanese Embassy in Kensington, and during the interval summoned Simon to his office. Ian knew that his Friday walk to the local for a drink with the boys must be sacrificed, as time was now of the essence. His spirits suddenly lifted and he began to whistle. Simon received his briefing from Ian, returned to his office and began to place various telephone calls. The immediate result was a breakfast meeting the following day with Rothschilds' Venture Capital, and lunch with Norman St John Associates, the international architects. The following week was a frenzy of activity as both Ian and Simon followed the Project Implementation Activity Schedule with targets reached, problems eliminated and goals achieved.

Overheard on the 7.15 a.m. Sevenoaks to Charing Cross later in the week was the remark, 'I say old chap, Ian's been wearing the same suit for the last three days. Do you think he has marital problems?' The question became a rumour and escalated around the tight-knit community of the 7.15 a.m. commuters.

Victor had called for a conference on the Sunday, ten days after the meeting with Kamal Bsat. Ian and Janette had been invited for lunch at Victor's Surrey residence. Simon would join them later. Ian had recently seen little of Janette but he had noticed that her normal cheerful disposition had a slightly haunted edge on those few occasions when he had actually looked at her. He had passed it off as a 'woman's thing' and thought no more about it as his mind was reeling with the multitude of tasks still remaining to be accomplished. That Sunday morning, they had left little William with their immediate neighbour Charlie Getlucky, a Chartered Accountant by profession, who delighted in reading the *Financial Times* aloud to his two young children, Percy and Prucilla. He had confided in Ian one Friday evening that his children were always occupied. What with homework or some other boring task, his special treats for then were usually limited to Sunday afternoons immediately after lunch.

Ian and Janette left the 'close', content in the knowledge that little William was in safe and knowledgeable hands. They chatted easily as the Ford negotiated the lanes of Sevenoaks. As they approached the M25, Janette turned to Ian and said, 'I met Mrs Rumjum in Tesco's yesterday morning. I was trying to select a tube of toothpaste. You know what it's like with all those special offers. I really get so confused. She came up to me, put her arm around my waist and whispered, 'All men are bastards.' Then she walked away. I was quite nonplussed and so confused that I forgot all about the toothpaste and drove my trolley into old Mrs Black's backside just as she was bending over the frozen peas. I also had Mrs Ryan telephone the day before, and before I could utter a word, she said, 'We understand how you must feel. You can always count on our support.' Then she put the phone down! You know that every Wednesday the milk bill must be paid. Normally our young milkman is very brisk and efficient, and it's all over in five seconds. This Wednesday he lingered. He actually suggested that he wouldn't mind a cup of tea or something, and asked if he could come in. I'm at a total loss to understand what is happening,'

Ian coughed, 'How peculiar,' he said in a rather strangled voice. 'Did you give him the cup of tea?'

'No, of course not. What would the neighbours think?' Janette retorted.

The Ford was eating up the miles as they sped sedately along the M25, debating the reason for the unusual events that had occurred to Janette the previous week. They turned off the motorway at the Leatherhead slip road, drove through Bookham, skirted Horsley and approached Guildford. Victor lived in large old farmhouse facing Clandon Park. In the seventeenth century when Victor's house was build, houses were referred to by the name of the field in which they were built. Victor's house had been built in a field called Longdicks. Previous owners; during the Victorian era, had changed the name to Longdyke. They drove up the gravel driveway towards the old house through a natural archway of mature trees. Janette spied squirrels playing in the branches, and the sound of chirping birds were almost as loud as the traffic roar on the M25. Longdyke was situated centrally in a three-acre plot. Other than a concealed garage where Victor stored his beloved Jaguars, it was hard to accept that central London was only forty minutes' drive away. The property had an atmosphere of tranquillity and homeliness that modern estate houses could never emulate. Well-manicured lawns surrounded the house on three sides. Flower beds were strategically placed, the chrysanthemums were in full bloom, the air was crisp and sharp in the warm autumn sunshine, albeit tainted with the savoury aroma of the countryside as deciduous trees prepared themselves for winter. They parked outside the five-bar farmhouse gate, on the gravel drive where it ballooned out into an enormous parking area. During the journey, neither Ian nor Janette had fathomed the reasons for the peculiar behaviour of their friends and neighbours, not least the milkman.

Victor stood at the open front door to greet them as they walked up the uneven stone-paved pathway, whose irregular joints were green with moss, giving the impression of a narrow giant jigsaw, 'One hopes that your journey was pleasant and one is delighted to welcome you to one's humble abode,' Victor amiably said as he kissed Janette on the cheek and then shook Ian's proffered hand.

They had previously been to Longdyke on numerous occasions and Victor always had the same greeting. He ushered them through the low, beamed inner hall, through the maze of low-ceiling corridors into the drawing room with its massive inglenook fireplace and small oak windows with views over the rear garden.

'What a delightful house you have, Victor,' said Janette.

'One is always appreciative of one's guests' pleasures,' uttered Victor. 'You must remind me over lunch to tell you the history of the old place. It really is quite fascinating.' Both Ian and Janette knew the history of Longdyke, as it had been recounted to them on many occasions previously.

At that moment Marjory Walpole popped her head round the massive jamb of the drawing room door. Marjory Walpole was a big woman, with thick iron-grey hair cut short around a rather elongated head. She had rather a high-pitched voice which she used to emit fragmented groups of words punctuated with rather long pauses, rather like Morse code. 'Oh, darlings... how wonderful to see you both... It's been years... You look so well... Hope you are... hungry, Victor?... You silly old fusspot... Our young guests are... dying for a drinky-poos... Well, not literally dying, of course... Ha ha.'

Ian and Janette settled themselves comfortably into the soft chintz sofa as Victor vanished to get refreshments, whilst Marjory chatted away, pausing constantly as if she were on the brink of succumbing to an asthma attack. Lunch was held in the old dining room. The beams in this room were so low that Ian could not stand erect. It was for that reason that it had been selected as the dining room, as guests could remain seated in comfort without the necessity of any vertical physical movement other than that normally displayed by a diner. Lunch was a jovial affair. Victor again recounted the history of Longdyke as Marjory discussed, mainly with herself, the trials and tribulations of keeping good help. Both would vanish at intervals to replenish the food and/or top up refreshments. Ian and Janette's contribution to the general conversation was generally muted, due, in part, to Marjory's insistence that they must have additional helpings of the delicious roast beef and second helpings of Yorkshire pudding. All their energy was confined to consuming the vast quantities of food and drink offered to them, whilst Victor and Marjory conducted separate dialogues on their favourite subjects. Victor, having related the history of Longdyke, had embarked on the history of the Jaguar motorcar, whilst Marjory was telling Janette about her varicose veins. Ian gave a sigh of relief and a slight belch as Simon's arrival was announced by the doorbell.

Marjory and Janette retired to the drawing room for coffee and chocolates, whilst the three men threaded their way through to Victor's study. The study was located at the back of the house and it had been furnished in a masculine style. Leather armchairs faced a massive oak desk and the walls were decorated with pictures of Jaguar cars. A pale blue Wilton carpet covered the floor, topped with Persian rugs laid in a seemly haphazard fashion. Along one wall was a floor-to-ceiling bookcase, jammed full of books, many being maintenance manuals on the various models of the Jaguar motor car. Victor waved Ian and Simon towards the direction of the armchairs whilst he seated himself behind the desk. Ian suddenly felt very tired; the room was so warm and quiet and the armchair moulded itself to his body as it offered supple support. His eyelids began to droop. Victor's voice cut through the gently forming mist.

'One is appreciative that one's guests have partaken of one's hospitality. Ian, would you be so kind as to acquaint us with the current state of play on Mr Bsat's little problem.'

Ian jerked his mind back into reality as he began to relate the results of the last ten days of frenzy. When he had finished, Victor smiled and said, 'Excellent. So we have achieved our principal objectives. That is to say, we have achieved a stay in the issue of the notice by the Lebanese Government, and Thomas Norman St John has agreed to conduct a full structural survey and prepare a preliminary design without charge, on the condition that, should the project proceed, his practice will be the appointed Design and Supervision Consultants. Thomas must understand that whilst one has no doubt that Mr Bsat will accept this condition, Thomas must be prepared to work in conjunction with a Lebanese architectural practice.'

Victor swivelled his body as he turned towards Simon. 'Now, young Simon, what is your progress?'

Simon had had a late night the previous evening. It was the young lady whom he had temporarily adopted for the evening who had shaken him at 10.30 a.m. on that Sunday morning, to remind him of his promise that they would go bungee jumping after breakfast as her reward. Simon had been obliged to explain that he was due in Surrey just after lunch and, quite frankly, his stomach just wasn't up to throwing himself off the jib of a 100-foot tower crane. He felt ill. His young lady cuddled up to him, murmuring into his tousled hair, 'What shall we do instead?' Coffee was uppermost in Simon's mind as he stretched for his pyjamas bottoms. Chris, his flatmate, was making noises in the bathroom adjacent to Simon's bedroom, providing a clear indication that his Saturday evening had been spent in a similar fashion to Simon's, although by the sound of the noises coming from the bathroom, Chris had indulged to a far greater extent. By lunchtime Simon was feeling much more his old self, and his young lady had been placated by his promise to ring her that evening after his return from Surrey. She kissed him wetly on the mouth as he deposited her outside her Mayfair mews cottage at 1.30 p.m.

Simon turned his Golf GTi 16V towards the southeast and began motoring. Simon's report was equally impressive. Rothschilds were prepared to compile a business plan and already had received statements of interest from various financial institutions pending receipt of the Prospectus. In principle, providing finance for the reconstruction of the St George Hotel should not be too difficult, as the Hotel's pre-war reputation was well known by many of the more elderly directors of the institutions approached, as many of them had stayed there in their younger days.

Victor beamed, 'Excellent again. One is very pleased with the results of your hard labours. One considers that a celebration drink may be permitted prior to identifying the next series of objectives.'

Ian had listened to Simon's report with interest and was impressed by the manner in which he had approached the various problems, and also by the style in which he had discussed the requirements with the senior managers at Rothschilds, many of whom were older and more wily than Simon. Victor interrupted his thoughts as he placed a balloon glass containing a fine cognac at Ian's elbow. Simon had elected a small sherry and Victor had accommodated this wish. Victor resumed his seat, beamed at them both and began to explain the details of the settlement made by Mr Bsat to the unfortunate gentleman who had been the recipient of Mr Bsat's partially smoked cigar.

'Actually,' Victor concluded, 'the gentleman was quite relieved that Mr Bsat's cash settlement completely cancelled his stock exchange losses. Apparently he was dreadfully worried as it was his wife's money that he had been gambling with without her knowledge. Mr Bsat also threw into the settlement a totally new set of attire from the gentleman's own London tailors. One was greatly relieved that legal action was avoided.'

The conference continued in a relaxed and positive manner with Victor setting out the next set of prime objectives with Ian and Simon discussing and identifying interim milestones and the procedures to achieve these goals. By late afternoon the three men had concluded their discussions, and Simon was able to excuse himself for his return to London.

Simon stopped at the Shell Petrol station on the northbound carriageway of the A3 and, whilst his Golf GTi 16V was being topped up, made various telephone calls from his mobile. As he continued his journey into central London, he smiled to himself. It was clear from his brief conversation with the young lady from Mayfair that she had spent the afternoon resting and was now intent on resuming her relationship with Simon with renewed vigour. The whine of the highly-tuned engine increased as Simon gently pressed the accelerator pedal towards the floor.

Ian and Janette stayed for a late afternoon tea, chattering amicably with Marjory and Victor about the multitude of minor events influencing their daily lives. The ebb and flow of the conversation was again a little unbalanced as, confronted with an enormous chocolate cake, Ian and Janette, between mouthfuls, could only respond in muffled tones during those pauses permitted by Marjory or Victor, with the inevitable result that the carpet in front of them was quickly covered with wet cake crumbs. Marjory, with her captive audience, dominated the conversation like an express train rushing through stations towards its final destination. As soon as a decent interval had passed, after tea had been finished, Janette turned to Ian and suggested that they should commence making their way home, as she was concerned about little William's homework. The farewells at the front door of Longdyke were genuine, as it was clear that both Marjory and Victor were fond of Ian and his lovely wife, Janette.

As Ian lowered himself into the driving seat of the Ford, he slyly undid his trouser buttons. His stomach, released from the constraints of the waistband, burst forth, popping his lower shirt button. The button bounced off the interior face of the windscreen and vanished into the back seat area of the car. Ian quietly cursed but the relief was so great that his irritation was immediately submerged under the feeling of well-being. They drove back to Sevenoaks in companionable silence, each wondering what unexpected events would happen to Janette during the coming week. Janette collected little William from their immediate neighbour, Charlie Getlucky (who expressed his appreciation of William's silent attention during the afternoon 'reading') while Ian put the Ford away into the garage. They entered their home and Ian closed the front door on the world outside, muffling as he did so little William's screams of rage.

Chapter 4

Felicity stirred, nudged into semi consciousness by John's weight pressing down on the king-size bed in which she and John had slept that deep sleep from which awakening is so difficult. Beside her, set out on the bedside table, was a large teapot under it's cosy, containing Harrods' 'Early Morning Brew' together with a milk jug and a cup already full of tea. John bent over his wife, pressed his lips into the tangled mass of hair, uncertain as to what he would encounter, and by chance brushed the lips of her full mouth, albeit askew. Leaning back he murmured, 'Darling, it's 6.00 a.m. I must be off otherwise I'll be stuck in traffic for most of the morning. Have a lovely day, and don't forget to drink your tea.'

The slamming of the apartment door and the receding sound of John's footsteps down the communal stairs (the lift was again not working) brought Felicity back into the reality of a new day. She stretched luxuriously in the warmth and comfort of the soft surroundings like a chrysalis safe in its cocoon. Reluctantly propping herself up with pillows stacked under her head, she reached for the first of a series of cups of tea. She had time to linger and her mind gradually began to focus. She glanced out of the bedroom window. It was going to be another beautiful day. The sky was cobalt blue with the early morning sun just peeping over the mountain range forming a rapidly dissipating bright halo over the jagged peaks of the impenetrable black mass below. Soon her actions became more coordinated as the caffeine took effect. She rose from her bed to commence the early morning chores. By 7.30 she was fully alert and ready to depart for Westwood Academy, the school where she taught English to her young Lebanese pupils. She collected her books, shut the apartment front door and began to follow John's recent descent down the apartment staircase. Pausing on the third floor, she exchanged early morning pleasantries with her young, newly married neighbour, Salwa Sawya. Salwa dutifully visited the village bakery every morning to procure for her husband's breakfast the newly baked Arabic unleavened bread. The bakery was a popular early morning venue where the villagers would congregate, still dressed in their night attire, but with dressing gowns over as protection against the cold. They would huddle around the baker as she rolled the raw wet dough into a ball followed by a whirling action as the dough was flung into the air, spinning it between her hands so that centrifugal force would elongate and flatten the rounded shape into a flat disc, which was then laid on top of a dome-shaped heated element to bake. The smell of baking bread was tantalising. Later, in the privacy of their own homes, the villagers would fill the bread with a central filling of cheese, jam or vegetables, the outer edges rolled around the central filling to form a multilayered cylindrical roll. Accompanied by Arabic coffee, it was delicious.

Felicity threw her briefcase into the back of her Jeep Cherokee, sat herself comfortably in the driver's seat and turned on the ignition. The four-litre engine roared into life and she let it idle whilst she adjusted her Alice Band. Out of the corner of her eye, she espied the procession of early morning shoppers, like sleepwalkers sheepishly threading their way to and from the bakery. She engaged drive and gradually depressed the accelerator of the powerful vehicle. John had bought her a Golf GTi on her arrival in Lebanon on the principle that it was small and powerful. The cut and thrust of the traffic had terrified her at first and she had refused to drive the little vehicle. The Golf had been traded in for the Jeep and, as she now sat above the level of most other motor cars, she looked down at the frantic antics of the heaving mass with contempt as she thrust the big nose of her vehicle directly into the path of a little Honda. The squealing of brakes and hooting of horns accompanied her passage across the T-junction as she made her way out into the main street and up the hill towards Westwood Academy. She turned left on to the slip road into Monteverde, and descended into the small valley containing large residential buildings, recalling, as she did so, the very first time they had used that road.

Mansourieh was a typical mountain village containing all those shops necessary to support community life. Centrally located in the village was a second-hand car dealer, Rouad, who traded in reasonable quality second-hand vehicles, generally imported from abroad. John had negotiated with Rouad a trade-in value for the Golf in part exchange. None of Rouad's current selection of vehicles appealed to Felicity, and Rouad had advised, through an interpreter, that his next shipment was due in Lebanon the following weekend and that they should return then. Both Felicity and John had returned on the prescribed date and after much debate, had selected from Rouad's gleaming assortment of imported second-hand vehicles a 1989 midnight blue Jeep Cherokee which, although rather battered, seemed to suit Felicity's needs. It was agreed that Rouad would have the vehicle overhauled, as he warranted his vehicles for six months, and that they should come back the following Saturday to collect their Jeep. They had faithfully returned the following Saturday, only to be informed by Rouad that the selected vehicle wasn't a good example. Could they come back in two weeks' time when he was anticipating a further shipment? John had wondered afterwards whether during the translation he had missed something. The negotiations had been accomplished with half the population of the village chipping in, so he thought it unlikely. They had faithfully returned to Rouad's again after his next shipment and this time had selected a 1989 black Cherokee whose condition was a substantial improvement on the previous one. Rouad again promised that he would have the vehicle overhauled and would they come back the following Saturday... On the due date, both Felicity and John arrived at Rouad's full of anticipation. Rouad greeted them warmly and advised that the vehicle they had selected had proved a poor example and that he was very sorry but he wasn't prepared to sell it to them. He was expecting another shipment in a couple of weeks, and would they return then? During these discussions, again seated in Rouad's spartan office, sipping Arabic coffee with the showroom cluttered with onlookers from the village, John explained that he thought that Rouad was a car dealer and that his business was selling cars. Rouad smiled at him and gestated that he didn't understand the question. 'Come back in a couple of weeks when I will have a really nice example for you,' he had said, through one of the many interpreters present.

John and Felicity had returned to the apartment a little confused. Felicity had mentioned during their journey that she thought she had seen their 'selected' Cherokee being driven through the village on Friday, looking very nice and going like a bomb. They had concluded that Rouad had over-valued the Golf, as trade-in and rather than lose face, had adopted the policy of 'unsuitability' for his popular British neighbours. John considered this explanation plausible, as the fact remained that Rouad would not sell them a vehicle. He appreciated that the village community was tightly knit and that the villagers had showed considerable kindness to their only British inhabitants. One of their most recent gestures was a gift of a two-litre bottle of home made Arack. Felicity had used the contents to clean the brass as it had been established, by accident, that the liquid contained similar properties to paint stripper.

Later that same afternoon they had gone exploring and had discovered, much to Felicity's delight, a superb example of a 1989 Jeep Cherokee in the mountain village of Baabdat, which they promptly purchased after a trial run. Not believing his luck, John had negotiated a trade-in value for the Golf in excess of his original purchase price. He left a deposit and was asked to return the following Saturday to give sufficient time to enable the dealer's garage to thoroughly overhaul the vehicle. Felicity had accompanied John on the agreed day to collect the Jeep. The first hint of trouble was the trade-in value negotiated on the Golf. A series of renegotiations were necessary due to the dealer's apparent misunderstanding as to what had been agreed. With the renegotiations concluded, John and Felicity had followed the dealer to his garage. They had travelled the narrow backstreets of Baabdat, finally emerging onto a deserted road leading to a valley. A solitary house stood amongst the tiered farmland, in amongst the olive trees and orchards of fertile Lebanon. As they pulled up alongside an evil-smelling pond, the croaking of the bullfrogs immediately ceased. They followed the dealer into a ruined barn adjoining the property, and behind their retreating backs, the chorus of croaking was resumed. There, in the interior gloom, was their Cherokee Jeep, in various bits and pieces spread all over the ground. They were obliged to return later that same day to the 'Garage' to take delivery of their splendid vehicle. Initially, the vehicle went well, bounding up the mountain slopes with a deafening roar. John had difficulty negotiating some of the hairpin bends on their way down to Mansourieh, as the steering seemed sluggish. They breasted the crest of the hill by the Trusty Supermarket and began the final descent into Mansourieh. The steering by this time was almost uncontrollable and John took the quiet slip road into Monteverde.

Half a mile past the Monteverde turn off, two things happened simultaneously. Felicity rapidly uttered, 'Darling, did you see that wheel going past?' as the Cherokee shuddered to an abrupt halt, gouging the bituminous road surface with its exposed disc brake as the front offside wheel raced past, conducted a series of ever decreasing circles, and finally flopped flat onto the road, fifty metres in front of the disabled vehicle.

John had found the whole day very frustrating and his anger had been building up. He gave vent to his emotions. As if by some magical spell, the deserted road was soon full of local residents, some giving comfort to Felicity, others sympathising with John, but the majority either wheeling the rogue wheel back into place or scouring the road surface for the missing wheel nuts. One young hulk of a man produced, as if from under his coat, a pneumatic jack; and in the time it takes to blink an eye, they had the Cherokee jacked up and were bolting on the wheel.

Fortunately the damage was slight, as it was only the front off side that had sustained a slight dent. With gratitude to the many willing helpers, John and Felicity said their good-byes and gingerly retraced their steps to the gloom of the 'Garage' at the back of beyond, near Baabdat. Their arrival was announced by the immediate cessation of the croaking of the bullfrogs. Fortunately the 'Garage' was still open, although the interior gloom was deeper now. Various telephone calls were made on the 'mobile' by the garage mechanic, and the dealer soon arrived. He was clearly shocked at the news of the incident, and at his insistence John and Felicity were ushered into the house where they were told to wait. Coffee was made and as they sipped it they looked out, through the dirty glass panes set in the rotting window frames, at the beautiful landscape of the valley as it dropped beneath them, illuminated by the redness of the setting sun.

As soon as the dealer departed, the bullfrogs resumed their chorus. Within half an hour he had returned, driving an almost new Mercedes 300 SLE. He explained, as he took Felicity's arm, that this was for her use until the Jeep was repaired. They were again requested to return the following Saturday to collect their vehicle. John and Felicity had laughed about the incident afterwards, their frustration tempered by the kindness shown. Every time Felicity travelled this stretch of road, the memories of that afternoon and the events leading up to it came flooding back.

She parked in the space reserved for teachers and entered the large villa, which had been converted into a school after its wealthy owners had leased it unconditionally to Westwood Academy. As she made her way through the spacious corridors, she stopped now and then to chat with various other young teachers whose arrival had preceded her own and who were busy preparing for the day's lessons. The villa was an annex to the main building. It served as a special unit for those children whose learning ability was impaired. In many cases the impediment was psychological due to their having been reared during the civil war. With patience and understanding these mental barriers could be dismantled, and the ability of the child exposed to the full effect of the school's excellent curriculum. Felicity had often been astounded by the capabilities of some of the children whom she had taught. Her current favourite was a little girl called Soha Hassam. Soha was small for her twelve years. She was the youngest daughter of one of Lebanon's most successful building contractors and she had come to the special unit due to her rather strange ability to write English backwards in a similar fashion to Arabic. Felicity immediately recognised that behind the large dark watchful eyes lay a remarkable talent. The course of that day was uneventful for Felicity, other than she was obliged to confiscate a 9mm automatic pistol from one of her young pupils. He had protested that it was quite safe, as his parents had not permitted him to bring the bullets! Felicity deposited the weapon with

Collette, the Director of the Unit. To the relief of all the teachers, it was Friday, and at the end of the school day they all departed for their respective weekend activities in buoyant mood.

★

Sami listen carefully to Mohammed as he crouched precariously in the bow of the small flat- bottom boat, shotgun ready. Sami had decided that he was due for a weekend shooting and had invited a few of the visiting Japanese delegation to accompany him. The Japanese Government were considering granting a soft loan of $150,000,000 to the Lebanese Government to assist in the reconstruction programme and Sami saw no reason not to cement friendships.

Lebanon is a physically divided country. The north-south flat coastal plain offers extensive access to the Mediterranean Sea. To the east lies the Lebanon mountain range, and then further still to the east, the Anti-Lebanon range, both parallel with the coastal plain. Between the two ranges lay the flat fertile Bekaa valley, the breadbasket of Lebanon. To the South of the Bekaa valley lies the Lac de Qaraoun. The passage of migrating wildfowl was over the Bekaa valley, and Sami knew that during certain times of the year, the sport was excellent. His guests, armed with their cameras and camcorders, had refused his offer of sporting rifles and shotguns. Sami mentally shrugged to himself that if his guests preferred to shoot with their own equipment that was their decision. He glanced at the small flotilla of boats, gently bobbing up and down on the rocky water. He had told Mohammed to arrange the hire of three boats, one for himself and two for his guests. Mohammed had made the arrangements but to their consternation one of the boats had developed a leak immediately after casting off. The Japanese were all crammed into one boat and its gunwales were perilously close to the water surface.

The day had not started auspiciously. Mohammed had collected the guests from their hotel in Sami's black Range Rover en route to collect Sami. One of the delegates, who had originally declined the offer, had changed his mind, and on arrival at Sami's villa, the car was full. Sami had been obliged to travel in his ancient Mercedes. The roads over the mountain pass, down into the Bekaa and then along the flat valley floor to the Lac de Qaraoun, had suffered years of neglect; the old Mercedes rocked and rolled along the uneven patched bitumen surface, the defective exhaust making conversation impossible. By the time they had reached their destination Sami had a headache and his mood was less than convivial. Out of the corner of his eye, Sami espied movement on the water. He brought his gun to bear and fired both barrels. The solitary wild duck, frantically paddling his way towards flight, suddenly gained additional momentum and soared into the air as Sami was reloading. Fortunately, just as Sami was aiming for his next pot-shot, a cry from the neighbouring boat distracted him and his shot went wide. The duck, fully into his airborne escape, quacked continuously as he rapidly receded into the distance. Sami turned towards the sound of the cry. One of his guests had overbalanced and gone overboard and was now standing neck deep in the water, his hair plastered to his head as his companions yelled encouragement, to which he replied in his own language. By noon, the day's sport had been abandoned. The unfortunate guest had been hauled aboard Sami's lighter boat. They had then landed and Mohammed had driven the sodden guest, still uttering explosive vocabulary in Japanese, to the nearest hotel, where they all subsequently adjourned for lunch. Sami had at last the opportunity to hear what Mohammed had been trying to say to him all morning.

Sami had instructed Mohammed to visit the various war-damaged buildings in 'Down-town Beirut' and to identify any building containing 'carved features'. Sami had obtained from the Council of Development and Reconstruction a detailed survey of the massive site. In all, 220 existing buildings were marked as scheduled for renovation, and Mohammed was to visit every one. Due to the precautions adopted by the Government against theft of materials and unauthorised occupation by squatters, the Lebanese Army maintained close guard over the whole area. The inspection was, therefore, to be clandestine and done at night. Mohammed had visited twenty buildings within the first forty-eight hours following the meeting and had reported his findings.

Sami had selected Mohammed for his ability to compile lists. Mohammed had a talent for lists. He would compile a list for every occasion and on those infrequent visits to Mohammed's apartment, Sami had been obliged to wade through piles of discarded paper, each representing a list. As Mohammed's memory was not what it once was, he would sometimes forget that he had already compiled a list on a particular subject or forgotten where he had left it, and he would then compile another list to replace the one he had either forgotten or misplaced. Sami required a list of all the buildings containing carved features. Sami had not anticipated the magnitude of the task and at Mohammed's current rate of production (ten dwellings a night), a full list would not be compiled in sufficient time. Sami had allowed for the contingency that Mohammed would either lose or misplace one of his lists, despite instructions that the results of each night's survey must be handed to Sami the following day.

Lunch was a dismal affair, although the Japanese apparently enjoyed it. They took it in turns to photograph one another wearing the fez and smoking the arguileh. Sami had provided entertainment but the belly dancer was past her prime. Her gyrations were accompanied by the creaking of protesting ligaments, and the colour of her complexion became quite ashen. Sami was pleased when his guests announced that they should return to Beirut as they had an important meeting the following day.

The return journey was uneventful, other than it took considerably longer than the outward one. It was accomplished in virtual silence as the Japanese guests became very quiet. Sunday is traditionally the family day with lunch, the priority, eaten at one of the many excellent Lebanese restaurants scattered throughout the country. Family reunions occur over lunch and the restaurants bulge with customers. The consumption of alcohol at these gathering is in inverse proportion to the consumption of soft drinks, notwithstanding that 50% of the population are Moslems. The public highways on a Sunday afternoon are very dangerous places. It takes a cool driver or an inebriated one to transverse the pitted roads amongst the unpredictable motion of the numerous vehicles swaying and weaving as they each conduct their own individual Grand Prix race on their homeward journey. Mohammed was in his element, bouncing off one car and rebounding onto another. He reached the hotel in Beirut, disembarked his passengers, who feeling terra firma beneath their mud-encrusted shoes, regained confidence and with it their joie de vivre'. Sami left the delegates bowing and bobbing with the knowledge that whatever impressions he had of the day's sport, his little friends had regarded it as an unforgettable experience. He could count on their cooperation. Sami returned to his villa with Mohammed in tow. Later that evening, Sami telephoned Omar and Ali.

★

Michael Fleming shouted obscenities at the taxi driver. The man grinned, gunned his old Mercedes, and in a cloud of blue-black smoke which enveloped Michael, vanished down a side alley. Michael coughed as he regarded the new dent on his Mini Moke with disgust. He had spent the day relaxing at the Club Sportive, immediately off Rass Beirut. Michael enjoyed his Sundays. The Club Sportive was the favoured place for the young set. A few beers, a sun lounger and a couple of beautiful girls to chat to. What more could any man want? he would tell himself. Michael was one of life's Romeos. His blond wavy hair crowned a majestic head mounted serenely on broad shoulders tapering seductively into an athletic figure. Six months in Beirut had trimmed his torso. The sunshine had done the rest. Michael was British, and the dark Lebanese girls loved him. Michael loved to be loved. He had assembled the Mini Moke from a car kit imported from England only six months ago. His many friends had ridiculed him about this mode of transportation but Michael was unrepentant. He had calculated that it would be his 'statement' to Beirut and he had proudly taken to the road only a month previously. This was his fourth dent and already the bright red paintwork was showing deep battle scars. 'I must increase the wheel diameter,' Michael thought. 'Perhaps then these bloody taxi drivers will see me...' He had got the idea from a Jeep Wrangler which, mounted on lorry-size wheels, had overtaken him. It would be a bit like a moon buggy, but what the hell!

Michael was a marine engineer engaged in the reconstruction of the Beirut International Airport. 'Always in deep water,' he would chuckle to himself, when some inquisitive stranger asked him his occupation. He had arranged that evening to play bridge with Mike Brady, and John and Felicity. 'The bloody car won't go,' he muttered to himself as he contemplated the crinkled mudguard. 'Suppose I'll have to get a bloody taxi and arrange to get this thing towed to the nearest garage. Bet there's a cartel – one guy smashes you up and his chum comes along later for the fare.' Amongst the background noise of passing traffic, a loud hooting became dominant and Michael glanced in the general direction of this sound. To his amazement he saw a slender hand attached to a willowy arm protruding from the open window of a large black Mercedes 500SE, beckoning him. '…I say, this looks promising…' he thought, as instinctively he groped for his comb.

Dania, seated in her father's parked car had witnessed Michael's accident and observed his subsequent actions. He's British, she thought to herself and a plan for that evening's entertainment rapidly formed in her fertile mind. Dania had been born in Beirut of Lebanese parents, but with the onset of the problems the family had relocated to London where her father's international business ventures had prospered. Dania had received the best English education that money could buy, finally finishing it in Switzerland. On her return to her parents' house in South Kensington, she had entered the London social whirl with such gusto that her parents saw less of her than previously. She loved London and her friends were many. Her parents, however, had other plans, and despite her vigorous protests, she had been flown back to Beirut to the family apartment her parents maintained in Raouche, with instructions to find a husband of the same cultural background and religion as the family.

Initially Dania had found life dull in Beirut and the Lebanese men boring. She fretted for her London friends. The competition amongst the young ladies to entice eligible bachelors to commit themselves to marriage was intense, as due to the war, many sons of wealthy fathers had been packed off to Western countries to continue their education and some, preferring Western culture, had failed to return. The war had also denuded the country of less fortunately endowed males who had been either killed or maimed. The daughters had remained, other than a fortunate few, with the consequence that females outnumbered males by three to one. Dania had had success, but the affairs had lacked that special ingredient.

She was still watching Michael. As Michael approached the parked vehicle, his vision gradually expanded to include the arm and its attachment to the body. It was only on reaching the vehicle that he stopped and bent down to peer into the dark interior that his eyes encountered Dania. *Cor, what a bit of alright…* The thought, flashed into his mind as he checked out one of the most beautiful girls he had even seen, and his mind seized as he was transported back to London when Dania spoke, in that cultured, gentle tone found predominantly in a well-bred Kensington 'gal',

'Hi, I'm Dania. I'm waiting for my friend Joumana. I saw your accident and wondered whether you needed a lift or something.'

Michael boggled at the suggestion of 'or something', but he instinctively switched to charm mode and Joumana's return to the car went unnoticed for a time, as the conversation between Dania and Michael became exclusive to them.

Michael telephoned John later that afternoon regretting his inability to attend their planned bridge session that night, but his accident had caused his immobility and something urgent had since cropped up…

Dania popped another Turkish Delight into Michael's mouth as he replaced the telephone receiver.

During his preoccupation on the kerbside with Dania, Michael had failed to notice the heavily loaded Range Rover with ashen Japanese faces regarding him from the side windows, not daring a frontal view of the obstacles ahead, as their vehicle raced its way along the pavement thereby avoiding the worst of the congested traffic. The driver was concentrating hard on the road, and he was followed by an aging Mercedes, driven by a single driver, a large bulk of a man with a grim countenance, who appeared to be talking to himself.

★

Ali and Omar entered Sami' s study. Copious pieces of paper lay scattered around the floor and they shuffled carefully through the lists, confining their steps to those pieces of exposed carpet, like islands in a treacherous sea, towards the hard chairs lined up against the wall. Omar had closely followed Ali and once when the island space was inadequate for them both, Omar had overbalanced, clutching, as he fell, at Ali' s jacket. The tearing of the material was a small reminder of their potential fate if the cache was not found. Sami had already threatened that he would personally tear them limb from limb. They reached their destination, sat and waited for Sami in silence. Their research was not proceeding well and this, the fourth meeting, boded ill as neither had managed to further their previous results.

Ali was getting bored with the constant questioning of old Salim's family. His frequent visits were enlivened by one of old Salim's granddaughters, who at twenty-five, was making suggestions that made his concentration wander. The family lived in one large room and, other than the parents, the children comprised four unmarried girls, the youngest being nineteen. Ali found it was difficult to be ruthless amongst the drying female underwear and the doe-eyed looks of the girls. Every time Ali visited, he brushed his head against brassieres hung out to dry on the internal clothes-line which stretched from wall to wall of the single room. Ali had a weakness for brassieres. He imagined what was normally inside them. Omar, having completed his list of streets and buildings within a 500 metre radius of the St George Hotel had been assigned to match these with the fragments still legible in the ledger. He had found no match, and Sami had widened the search to, 1,000 metres and then to 1,500 metres. He was tired. His daytime duty as a tour guide was no longer in demand as the majority of hotels were empty. He was obliged to supplement his meagre income by 'waiting' at the Modca Cafe, off central Hamra, and the hours for waiters were long and the tips poor. His family of twelve put pressure on him and he had long ago lost the belief that parenthood was God's gift.

The study door opened slowly as Sami, talking to some concealed person, delayed his entry into the room. His deep voice growled and snarled in response to a lighter murmur. Clearly Sami had not had a good day, as with the end of the conversation, he thrust his body through the opening and slammed the door behind him. He glared at his captive audience and, heedless of the paper festooned around the floor, arrowed his way to the table at the opposite end of the room to face the chairs supporting Ali and Omar. He lowered himself behind the table onto a soft chair and began to rummage in the piles of paper covering the tabletop, grunting as he did so, 'What further news do you two have? It had better be good, I'm in no mood for more excuses. Ali, what have you got to tell me?'

Ali swallowed and hesitantly began to recite the latest information. Sami interrupted, 'This is what you told me last week! What further progress have you made?' Ali kept swallowing.

'Omar,' Sami barked, 'what's your contribution?' Omar fumbled with his shoelace. 'Omar!' Sami roared, 'What have you achieved since the last meeting?'

Omar's voice faltered and went up an octave. His lips moved and out jumped a squeak. 'The family are hungry. I have to work in the day – and then again at night!'

Sami sat back in the soft chair, and the sides billowed out as his towering height decreased in proportion to the expanding sides. He had forgotten to support Omar's family. It had been four weeks since the initial meeting and the result to date had been disappointing. He silently regarded his two henchmen as his mind began to assimilate the information obtained. Were there any clues that he had missed in the pile of information? He was convinced that his approach was correct. It was only the elimination of the impossible that would produce that which was possible. Once the possible had been identified, they could focus their attention. What I need, he concluded, is a policeman. With that thought in mind he picked up the telephone and dialled a number.

Chapter 5

The International Time Zone precluded simultaneous actions, but by coincidence, various people checked their calendars at the same time on the same day.

The progress on the St George Hotel brief was reaching a new milestone. Ian and Simon were scheduled to fly to Beirut next month for various meetings with an eminent Lebanese advocate. Thomas Norman St John was to accompany them. Simon checked his calendar to firm up his work schedule prior to their anticipated departure.

Ian, in buoyant mood and in the sanctity of his own office, checked his calendar as his excitement mounted. He was impatient for the departure date. The intervening days seemed long and boring, notwithstanding that they were eventful and full of purpose. The regulars on the 7.15 Sevenoaks to Charing Cross had viewed Ian's recent behaviour with silent disapproval. Gone was the regular conservative attire, as Ian had taken the final plunge into depravity by purchasing a couple of floral ties that now adorned his person, together with fluorescent socks.

Paul James rapidly thumbed through his diary, checking various dates against his work calendar. He concluded that the less important meetings must be delegated to his second in command, if he was to leave his work 'ship shape' for his successor. His appointment with Murhead International had been confirmed early that month with a financial package that he had found irresistible. He confessed to himself that he was looking forward to the challenge of the new position which promised to be arduous; but in the interim he disciplined himself to concentrate on his current duties.

Samantha brushed the crumbs of the jam doughnut from her full sensuous lips with a pale pink silk handkerchief, musing as she did so about her pending holiday. She had planned to go skiing with her flatmate, Charlotte, and they had already paid a deposit for a 14-day package tour to New England, USA. Charlotte had been having an affair with a young barrister, Robert MacIntosh, who, unknown to Charlotte had embarked on a cookery course at his local technical college due to Charlotte's culinary capabilities being confined to low carbohydrate meals. He had lost weight during the affair and his mother had insisted, rather strongly, that he must eat proper meals. Unless he was prepared to take positive action she would move into his apartment to look after him. Faced with this ultimatum, Robert had enrolled in the evening course, being the less odious option, with the consequence that his available time with Charlotte was severely restricted. Charlotte, possessive by nature, suspected a diminishing of Robert's affection towards her, and had returned home to her Mum in tears. The whole holiday was in jeopardy. Samantha checked her calendar and the time remaining prior to their departure. Charlotte's current behaviour, Samantha thought, made her a disgruntled companion and she imagined the après-ski evenings spent listening to Charlotte's grizzling and groaning about Robert.

John rummaged through his files, found the one that Silver had given him, opened it and studied the various design and construction programmes contained therein. He paid special attention to the programme for Dwelling No 121. Renovation was scheduled to commence early next year. He checked his calendar. He had a little under fourteen weeks.

Victor contemplated his calendar reflectively and murmured, 'If one has the Daimler Jaguar serviced on the 15th, should one use the XK or the Mark 2?' Unable to reach a decision, he resumed his work.

Felicity examined her work programme. Next week she had been allocated forty periods of teaching. Her mandatory working week was thirty-three hours (thirty-three periods). She did some juggling with the aid of her calendar.

Sami was deep in conversation with Omar Zien. Omar was a retired policeman who had spent many years in the French police force as a detective. Sami glanced at his calendar and they agreed a date.

Kamal Bsat had only been awake for two hours. He had an appointment with his accountant later that morning. Over his breakfast, he had skidded through his monthly accounts and idly wondered what day fell on the 31st. He reverted to his Pirelli calendar, not so much to identify the day but in his idleness, to admire the monthly semi-naked beauty.

Samantha's subsequent discussions with Simon about their parents' apparent dilemma had waned, since Samantha's telephone conversation with her mother had partially reassured them both. Simon had been pre-occupied with his current project and Samantha had been busy, living her life to the full. Their communications since, although frequent, had been brief.

Simon telephoned his sister with the news of his pending visit to Beirut.

'Oh Simon,' exclaimed Samantha. 'You must be terribly excited about seeing Mum and Dad again!'

Simon had received a typical English public school education and, through his stiff upper lip, assented that he was. Their conversation was curtailed by an incoming international telephone call to Samantha. Dispensing with an inquiry from an unemployed company director, spending his generous redundancy payment in Marbella, with her usual efficiency, Samantha again resumed her contemplation of the skiing holiday. Mentally, she realised that she had already categorised it as potentially awful. What on earth, she thought, made her decide to go skiing with Charlotte? She was fond of Charlotte but considered her unstable at times of emotional stress. Her parents had often spoken in glowing terms of the skiing facilities in the mountains of Lebanon. She began to consider the possibility of changing her holiday plans. She reasoned to herself, that if Dad paid the airfare, it would be a more economical holiday, although she would miss the après-ski fun. She could always explain to Charlotte that her parents had asked her to come and visit. Her plans began to ferment and by the time she had placed a call to her mother in Beirut, she was quite heady with excitement. Many of the Lebanese boys were enamoured by the fair-skinned English girls, as they represented a total contrast to the dark-skinned Lebanese beauties. The possibility of a brief holiday flirtation established itself firmly in her mind.

Felicity adjusted her Alice band as the telephone in the lounge began its soft burring. Felicity's emotions were in turmoil. Her teaching periods entailed a brief introduction to Shakespeare, to add depth to her general English tuition. One of her pupils had developed a passion for Shakespearean speech, and although her sessions briefly embraced examples of some of the Master's plays, this particular pupil studiously learnt, by heart, all of the plays. His English speech was punctuated with 'thee', 'thou', 'shalt', 'ye' and similar 'olde worlde' words. They occurred in his written work, and no matter how hard Felicity tried to break the habit, it would reassert itself the moment her attention was diverted. He would parade around the school spouting speeches from *Macbeth, The Merchant of Venice* and many other plays. The other pupils were gradually ostracising him as his diction to them was incomprehensible. The responsibility lay with Felicity to bring him back into the fold. Samantha's quiet voice soothed Felicity, and soon the day's frustrations were overlaid with the excitement of planning Samantha's skiing holiday with them.

John returned early that evening to his apartment. It had been a quiet day and he was relaxed as he left his office. His day's work had been completed by mid-afternoon, and with time on his hands, he allowed the various schemes that had been developing in his subconscious to surface. His conscience told him that he must report his discovery to the appropriate authority. It was possible that he would be eligible for a reward. It was more probable that his contribution to the sudden wealth of a minor Government official would go unnoticed and unacknowledged. His normal ethical behaviour was taunted by his other side, expounding the personal benefits to himself and his family if he could only smuggle the gold out of the country. Until he could break the inner conflict inside him, he knew that all of his schemes were doomed. He had decided during the afternoon that he would confide in his old friends Michael Brady and Michael Fleming.

Sami's meeting with Omar (the detective) had gone well enough and he was reassured that matters would now progress at a more rapid rate than before. Sami had explained the problem to Omar as the two men sat comfortably in soft chairs, sipping Arabic coffee in Sami's spacious villa…

Sami's wife, Rania, had three brothers, and they had all inherited an equal part of their father's estate. The estate comprised a building in central Beirut, where the family lived for most of the year, and a villa in the mountains where they would reside during the hot summer months. They suspected that their father owned a separate building in downtown Beirut which he leased. One of the sons had been killed during the troubles and the other two had fled, one to Canada, the other to Australia, where they had made for themselves new lives. The family had lost all documentation proving their title to the family properties, other than the property in central Beirut. They were resigned to the loss of the downtown building which had, most likely, already been confiscated by the Government. The family always suspected that their father kept duplicate copies of deeds. The mountain villa had escaped damage and, although dilapidated, it was unoccupied. Despite extensive research and inspection of the central Beirut property (which Rania still owned), the family had been unable to discover any deeds which would prove title to the mountain villa. This Villa was not subject to forfeiture as it was beyond the curtilage of Beirut. Rania had recently discovered some of her father's old documents amongst a pile of old books which, it was thought, referred to the location of the downtown Beirut property. As there existed the possibility that duplicate copies of deeds may have been concealed in this building, Sami was anxious to locate the building and with the permission of the authorities, conduct a total inspection to establish if it contained anything that might support their title to the mountain villa.

Omar (the detective) heard Sami's explanation in silence. He was aware of Sami's reputation and knew that the family had had property. It was common with most Lebanese families to maintain a mountain villa as a summer home as well as having a main house in Beirut. The explanation was plausible, although Omar was suspicious. It was true that many records had been destroyed but he had not previously heard of insurmountable difficulties in proving title to properties. However, the fee offered was generous and Omar's pension was small. The cost of living in Beirut was high and the investigation would fill in his lazy days of retirement. He said nothing to Sami of his suspicions as he consented to do what he could in locating the 'downtown building'.

Sami had previously copied selected parts of the fragmented information contained in the old ledger and this was handed to Omar (the detective), together with the results of Ali's investigation and that of Omar's (the waiter) including their respective telephone numbers. The two men agreed that Sami's approach was probably correct and that Omar (the detective) would contact him in two weeks' time, or earlier, if he had positive results. With the matter concluded, Sami handed over a large retainer with a promise that the balance would be paid once the downtown property had been located. As Omar (the detective) was leaving Sami's villa, his mind was working rapidly. He knew that Sami had been a local warlord during the civil war and that the war effort had been funded personally by the respective warlords. He found the tale about the downtown property implausible and he suspected that it might contain more than a piece of paper proving title. He grinned to himself as a 'Service' taxi ground to a halt in front of him. He instructed the driver to take him to the Riviera Hotel where he intended to treat himself to his first decent meal for weeks. After all, he had all afternoon to sleep it off. Halfway through the excellent lunch, just as he started his second bottle of superb French wine, he had crystallised his thoughts and had decided that he should become a frequent visitor to the Riviera Hotel.

Michael Brady stared at his half empty glass of Almaza beer. 'Man, you must be joking!' he exclaimed as John fell silent. Michael was originally from Northern Ireland, a large craggy man with a granite face. Michael was formidable, but to those who knew him well, his disposition was gentle and his heart was made of gold. He had accepted, he admitted to himself, the position in Beirut on the rebound. His love was India, and he, his wife and their three young children had lived in Nepal for eight years. With the completion of the project he had returned to Belfast to the family home, but once the novelty of civilisation (as it was called) had worn off, he began to pine for adventure in an environment to which he could relate. Michael was a telecommunications expert, and whilst employment opportunities abounded in Belfast for people of Michael's ilk, he was unable to reconcile the savagery of Northern Ireland with the gentle and caring attitude of the inhabitants of the wild and vast province of Nepal. His depression deepened as exposure to the media bombarded him with the latest outrage perpetuated by the IRA. It was in this state of mind that he applied for an accompanied position in Saudi Arabia, reasoning to himself that the vast empty desert would offer solace to his soul during his leisure time. Political events affecting the project prevented early confirmation of his appointment, and in desperation he had accepted an unaccompanied position in Beirut as Project Manager on a large telecommunications project to be executed on behalf of the Lebanese Government. For his first three months he hated Beirut. Gradually, as he fought the loneliness of single status existence, he began to perceive, under the entrepreneurial veneer of the Lebanese, the warmth and hospitality of the real people, which – considering the deprivations they had suffered during fifteen years of civil war – astounded him. He began to respond. His hostile attitude mellowed as his friendships deepened. Every Sunday he would drive up into mountainous areas of Lebanon to savour the isolation and wildness of the inhospitable landscape which breathed new spirit into his large frame. He had also become firm friends with John and Felicity.

'That's not a constructive comment,' John retorted. They were seated in a dark corner alcove in the Hare & Hounds 'English' pub, located near Mansourieh. The pub was half-full with expatriates quietly chatting to casual friends made in the bar. The atmosphere was smoke-laden and the consumption of beer was such that the bartender had difficulty replenishing the profusion of proffered empty glasses.

'Jesus,' Michael said after a pause, 'I think you should buy me another while I think this through.' In the solitude of the alcove, Michael sat meditating on John's discovery. Oh man, he thought to himself, what do you do with forty bags of gold sovereigns?

Professional minds are excellent at competently accomplishing the difficult tasks within the framework of their training and even a little beyond. But this was something quite different, and neither Michael nor John had any experience relating to it. Michael conceded that it was necessary to break the conflict between professionalism and self-interest. That was their real problem. Their debate continued long into the night as the pub filled up and then gradually emptied.

Omar (the detective) was making progress. He reasoned that (1) he knew the locality of the building in downtown Beirut; (2) he had fragments of the building's name, and (3) he had fragments of the street name. All that was necessary was to examine the old records of down-town Beirut and identify those buildings containing the known letters against the streets also containing the known letters. Within seven days, he had identified four buildings that corresponded with the fragmented information in his possession. A survey of those buildings should produce his due reward. During his investigation he had frequented the Hotel Riviera each day and the contents of his dustbin was illustrative of his new taste. Empty whisky bottles now replaced the poor quality plastic carrier bags of the street vendor. On the eighth day, Omar (the detective) died. The post-mortem showed alcoholic poisoning. He left no notes, and the results of his investigations went with him. He had not been in contact with Sami. Sami received the news of Omar's (the detective) death with unconcealed fury. Slamming the telephone receiver hard against its cradle, the instrument snapped in two. This only exacerbated his anger and the interior of Sami's villa echoed all morning with muffled oaths and the sound of splintering wood.

Ian and Simon compared notes. Thomas Norman St John Associates had completed their structural survey and a copy of this, together with a preliminary concept design for the renovation of the St George Hotel, lay in two bound volumes on Ian's desk. The indicative construction cost together with a preliminary layout for the interior design and furniture, fittings and equipment schedule had been defined and conveyed to Rothschilds. They had incorporated the information into the feasibility study accompanying the Prospectus and the document had been circulated to interested investors. Replies were trickling in. Murhead International had made a firm capital commitment (subject to contract). Quentin Lloyd of Rothschilds had already confided in Ian that, in his opinion, the committed capital would exceed that which was required. The flight had been booked and hotel reservations made. They were due to depart for Beirut on the 2nd January. Simon had requested that he should be allowed to precede Ian by a week so that he could spend Christmas with his parents. Victor, in jovial mood in the run-up to Christmas, had consented.

Beirut, in the days before Christmas oozed seasonal goodwill. The motoring community, cocooned in their stationary vehicles, smiled as dancing Santa Claus figures accosted the vehicles en masse. The tinny ding-dong of little bells held by these Santa Clauses could barely be heard above the din of tooting horns and revving engines as the traffic sought any avenue of escape from the traffic gridlock. A casual observer could see the escalating moods within the stationary vehicles as, whilst frustration was tempered with goodwill, the constant assault by the Father Christmases gradually created a feeling of despair and hopelessness as the drivers inched their way towards their respective destinations. The chatting policemen on point duty had long ago discarded any semblance of traffic control and could be seen, perched high on their central island podiums, draped in tinsel and flashing fairy lights. The shop display windows, festooned with artificial snow, sported reindeer and snowmen along-side merchandise for sale, adding to the excitement of a bustling, although stationary city. The sun overhead smiled on Beirut whilst the blue sky showed no emotion other than tranquility. Sons and daughters, conscious of their duty to the family, scoured the markets, the commercial centres and the roadside vendors' stalls in their quest to satisfy family expectations at minimum prices, as at every function it would be expected that the guests would bring a gift for the host, and their families were large. Many gifts must be procured, not least for the little ones.

Mountain villages did not escape the festive season, and in Mansourieh inflatable Santa Clauses, tethered to electricity pylons, bobbed up and down in the wind. The festivities were not without their hazards as one life-size Santa Claus, breaking free from his moorings was seen heading down the one-way road system (the wrong way), at a healthy rate of knots, causing immense traffic congestion as the weary motorists, elated by their triumph in escaping from Beirut, took evasive action to avoid the descending festive figure – invariably into the neighbouring vehicle. The rogue Santa Claus left in his wake a turbulent sea of broken glass and dented vehicles, but animosity between drivers was slight as the majority laughed at the rapidly diminishing figure coursing his way down the mountain road in a series of vertical hops towards the metropolis where, no doubt, he would create more chaos, confusion and merriment.

John had contemplated his gift to Felicity. He had discarded his original idea of presenting her with valuable antiques, which were generally manufactured in the month previous to Christmas and then subsequently subjected to various aging processes, including urination and burial. He had settled on an Egyptian card table as both he and Felicity were bridge players, and it would while away the evening in the companionship of friends. Felicity had contemplated John's present. She had also considered antiques but fortunately had discarded the idea as John was sensitive about his age. He might consider such a present a reflection of his advancing years. She settled on a leather waistcoat of European manufacture with the confident knowledge that the hide had been properly cured. She recalled the previous occasion when her Lebanese neighbour had presented her with a locally made furry leather bag. Their landlord had eyed the bag with suspicion as he related to her the fact that four of his pet cats had recently gone missing. Felicity had later given the bag a proper burial as the smell was becoming offensive.

She and John had decorated the apartment with the mandatory Christmas tree and all its accoutrements, paper chains and balloons until it resembled Father Christmas's grotto. Simon was after all going to spend Christmas with them.

Simon's flight had been relatively uneventful. He had caught the Middle East Airways flight departing Heathrow at 9.30 a.m. (local London time), arriving at 4 p.m. (local Beirut time). The approach to his destination was breathtaking as the aircraft descended to its final run in. He saw the towering mountains, dotted with tiny villages, flowing into the coastal plain, crowned with skyscraper buildings teetering on the edge of golden sands, with the blue Mediterranean Sea lapping at the edge. The whole scene was bathed in a golden light as the setting sun, on its way to bed, cast its benevolent smile over the world. Within thirty minutes of landing at Beirut International Airport, Simon had been reunited with his parents.

Chapter 6

Simon viewed his bulging Christmas stocking with resignation. He had many years previously seen through the deception of Father Christmas and his frantic activities on Christmas Eve to distribute the allocated Christmas present to millions of eager children. '...At 31 years of age...' he mused, '...surely Mum and Dad realise the futility of continuing this charade...?' But his parents strictly maintained their traditional role with their offspring despite pleas to the contrary. The multicoloured skiing sock was torn at the heel, the fragments of frayed wool an untidy fringe to the gaping wound from which appeared the corner of a gift-wrapped present. Simon regarded the two-dimensional printed image of Father Christmas's face who stared unblinkingly back at him. The ruddy face, framed with his bubbly white beard and capped with his red cap, was disfigured by a paper crease rendering the print almost deformed.

Christmas Eve had been hilarious. The journey from Beirut International Airport to his parents' mountain apartment had infused into Simon the Christmas spirit. Symbols of the festive season abounded everywhere and Simon found the atmosphere of goodwill irrepressible. It had started as Simon left the customs hall and entered no-man's land between the control area of the airport to the arrival lounge. An MEA ground hostess, a slender beauty, had approached Simon as he exited one area prior to entering the other, and with a soft voice brimming with Eastern promise, welcomed him to Lebanon and politely asked if, on behalf of Middle East Airways he would accept a gift with their compliments. Assenting that he would be delighted, she proceeded to kiss Simon on both cheeks prior to thrusting into his hand a small gift-wrapped box. With a fleeting smile she vanished to repeat the same welcome to the next emerging passenger. The arrival lounge was packed with local inhabitants waiting for the arrival of distant relatives, family or friends. Simon was awe struck as he emerged into the public area, confronted as he was by a sea of red bobbly hats each with white ball tassels mounted on bobbing heads. The festive headdress flowed down, in some cases, to dark beards, but it was the expression and general atmosphere that had the greatest impact on Simon. Smiling faces, all exhibiting excitement, surveyed the slim young man as Simon gently pushed into the joyful seething melee in search of his parents. A booming voice caught his attention. 'Simon, old boy, we're over here.'

Simon resisted the immediate think bubble of '...where the hell is over here...?' as the boom gave him direction like a foghorn provides to a passing sea vessel in dense fog. He soon saw his father dancing up and down but it was not until the crowd had parted sufficiently that he espied his diminutive mother. The following moments passed in an assortment of emotions, for it had been many months since their last reunion.

The return journey to his parents' mountain apartment had been uneventful. A couple of near collisions had not disturbed the animated conversation within the vehicle other than a few caustic remarks uttered by Simon's father. Their arrival outside the apartment had been accompanied by more caustic comments due to the multitude of parked cars and their inability to find a suitable parking space within the vicinity of the apartment. The lift was non-functional due to a power cut, although the standby generator quietly putted away in the background providing flickering illumination. As Simon ascended to the fifth floor, threading his way past wall-to-wall, ceiling-hung paper chains and squeaky balloons, he had the impression of entering a carnival haunted house, and his nerves tensed in anticipation of an illuminated ghoul figure suddenly confronting him as he continued his torturous journey.

Simon casually kicked the duvet off the double bed, approached the open window and stood staring out at the huddle of neighbouring apartments squatting beneath the majesty of the towering mountains. A warm breeze caressed his naked body with its soft invisible tentacles. The day had dawned bright and Mr Sun was saying 'Good morning' to those of the population who had roused themselves from their nest beds. Simon was in the prime of life. His muscles were well defined and rippled deliciously as he stretched to his full height of 6'1". The sound of movement in the adjoining areas of the apartment caught his attention and he quickly moved to the bedroom door, much to the chagrin of a young Lebanese woman hanging out the family washing over the interwoven mesh of telephone cables, festooned between apartments, to dry in the warmth of the early morning sunshine. Out of the corner of her eye, she had glimpsed a flash of white flesh at an adjacent window. Turning rapidly, she received the 'full Monty' view of a muscular torso surmounting a pair of muscular thighs. Her eyesight was keen and the memory would remain with her for some weeks constituting, as it would, the topic of conversation within the village – with a few embellishments.

Simon, burrowing into his suitcase, extracted an exotic polka-dot dressing gown, threw it casually across the back of his broad shoulders and manfully strode through the open bedroom door into the bowels of his parents' apartment. Crossing the lounge he approached the balcony. Felicity had already set out breakfast fare, and Simon's father was tucking into soft white rolls, still steaming from their recent delivery from the baker's oven. John had queued that morning at the adjoining bakery, clad, as was customary, in his worn dressing gown, feet thrust into dilapidated slippers. He refused to fully conform to custom and his semi-bald head was visible to any passing bird, pallid in comparison to the multicoloured bobble hats habitually worn by the early rising male population. His progress was clearly visible during the jostling for strategic queue positions.

Simon's conversation with his parents had generally been limited, since his parents' arrival in Lebanon, to intermittent telephone calls or on the occasional reunions, when the excitement of meeting had removed any inhibitions. He felt strangely nervous as he took his chair at the breakfast table. Slurping his coffee, his father greeted him gruffly, but with affection. Initially, conversation was halting as preliminaries were dispensed with and food and coffee consumed. Felicity had appeared halfway through the meal, cup of tea clutched in one hand, her hair cascading around her face notwithstanding the clothes peg gathering loose strands on to the top of her head. She, like Simon's father, was dressed in a faded dressing gown. Conversation gradually gathered momentum and soon Simon felt the intervening years of separation from his parents slipping away as if they had never existed and the comfortable feeling of a family relationship reasserting itself. At the foremost of Simon's mind was that nagging question, '…what's the old man up to…?'

The morning passed pleasurably, and it was early afternoon before an opportunity presented itself for serious discussions. Simon's parents, as usual, were having pre-Christmas lunch drinks. Simon, seizing the opportunity, confided in his parents the concern that he shared with Samantha. He was sufficiently perceptive to notice the look that passed between his parents as he broached the subject. His father, quietly sipping his drink, surveyed his son with respect. He had certainly not advertised the fact that he had discovered the hoard of gold and it must have taken an astute mind to fathom out that all was not as it should be. He contemplated silently whether he should share the secret with Simon, as he considered knowledge of that kind was dangerous. He looked towards Felicity for guidance. Felicity nodded slightly. Turning to Simon, he explained that what he was about to relate was very confidential and on no account must he repeat it to anybody. John needed that reassurance. Simon, assenting, leant back into the soft fabric of the chair as his father, in his well-modulated voice, narrated the sequence of events leading up to the discovery of the gold bullion. As if to consummate the tale, John reached into the folds of his dressing grown and passed to Simon a couple of gold sovereigns.

A multitude of questions flashed into Simon's mind. He had difficulty in prioritising them. 'What do you intend to do, Dad?' he eventually croaked.

His father replied, 'What would you do if you were in our situation?' Rapidly discarding notions of personal gain, Simon replied, 'From what you say, informing the authorities would only enrich the informed officials. You and Mum clearly have no interest in keeping any of this money, and if it is left undisturbed, it will be lost, buried under a couple of feet of concrete. Of course, there is the possibility that it may be accidentally discovered during the renovation works, but from what you have described about the reconstruction, that is unlikely.'

John agreed and replied, 'You haven't answered the question.'

'It's a bit difficult, Dad, I don't really know all the circumstances or the local situation.'

John appreciated the logic of his son's answer. John replied, 'The longer we live here, the more we become aware of the inequalities of Lebanese society. The gulf between rich and poor is vast. You only have to study the traffic to see what I mean. There are expensive Mercedes, Jaguars, Range Rovers and the like, rubbing bumpers with ancient jalopies. There is nothing in between. This wealth gap was exacerbated by the civil war, which brought with it misery on a scale that you and I could never even contemplate. It seems to us only right that money destined to create misery should be channelled into the creation of happiness. Your mother and I have discussed this at length, and we feel that every effort should be made to enable the Lebanese children to have a richer and more purposeful life. We feel that it should be for their future education so they may make a contribution to their own country. The problem is that corruption in Lebanon is endemic and we just don't know how to set about solving this problem.'

'Have you discussed this with the British Embassy?' Simon asked.

'No', his father replied, 'we have discussed it with very few people, and only those that we have confidence in. There may be real danger in the possession of this knowledge. I have no doubt whatsoever that the hoard is not forgotten, and that somebody somewhere in Lebanon is, at this very moment, actively seeking to recover the bullion.'

Sami Hassan jumped as the crack of the Christmas cracker startled him. Set out on the enormous table before him was a Christmas lunch consisting of a multitude of vast dishes. The food had been piled high, and it was of such gigantic proportions that those guests seated on the opposite side of the table were all but invisible. All that could be seen was a row of multicoloured

Christmas hats, bobbing and twisting in chaotic rhythm as the semi-concealed wearers, pausing in their animated conversation with their immediate neighbours, stopped to replenish their already distended mouths with more food. The room resonated with animated conversation, the occasional sharp crack of Christmas crackers, and a barely discernable dull clip-clop of silver utensils on china plates. The steady hum of chewing interspersed by the odd fluctuant baritone whistle, added to the informality of the occasion. Sami had invited his immediate family, relatives and close friends to celebrate Christmas with him. In all, fifty people sat around the table, noisily filling their bellies as they enjoyed Sami's annual hospitality. Sami took no part in the social chatter. He was preoccupied. He strongly suspected that Omar (the detective) had made progress in tracking down the bullion. It was unbelievably bad luck that he had died without leaving any clues. He suspected that the untimely death of Omar (the detective) had been brought on by his sudden lust for high living. Why, he reasoned, would he adopt this alien lifestyle unless he was confident that he would share in the proceeds of the bullion? Sami forced his mind back to recall the minutiae of his meetings with Omar (the detective). He had already made enquires about Omar's habits immediately after his death and had discovered that Omar (the detective) had been frequenting many of the downtown nightclubs. These nocturnal habits had commenced about ten days after his initial interview with Sami. Clearly, he had discovered something. Sami was acutely aware that time might be running short. He remained convinced that the bullion was secreted somewhere in the BCD district. Solidere, the developer, was rapidly executing construction work, and they had planned commencement of a new parcel of renovation works within the next few month. The more work they executed, the more the prospects of tracing the bullion diminished. He withdrew further into himself as the party raged around him.

Simon and his parents had enjoyed a traditional English Christmas lunch. The family tradition had no respect for country, and the Christmas tree, adorned with presents, offered the opportunity to continue with the festivities. Festooned in wrapping paper, Simon extradited himself to visit the bathroom. It was whilst the call of nature was answered that he had the seed of an idea. It gradually germinated within his fertile mind and as it blossomed he was certain that it was worth discussing with his father. His thought patterns were rudely shattered by a sudden thudding on the outside of the bathroom door.

'I say, old boy,' boomed his father's voice, 'are you alright? You've been in there for fifty minutes. I know Mum's cooking is a bit suspect, but I've never had the runs immediately after a meal.'

Simon reassured his father that he was fine. He had just been contemplating something and it had had nothing to do with Mum's cooking.

'Then could you come out, please,' his father requested. 'Mum's in the other loo, and I really feel it may be prudent if I have the opportunity to exercise the privacy of this one.'

In the solitude of the lounge Simon continued to examine his plan. 'Yes, damn it!' he exclaimed to himself. 'It should work,' he eventually concluded. Later that evening, Simon and his parents cloistered in the privacy of the apartment, talked late into the night and agreed to implement certain activities as soon as possible.

Sami dutifully kissed the cheeks of the last of his departing guests, without, as is the Arabic way, any distinction of gender. Silently, he objected to the new fashion of 'designer stubble', contact with stubble irritated his full lips. He stood in the open door to his villa watching the vast retreating bottoms waddle towards their parked Mercedes. It was with a sigh of relief when he closed the door and shut out the world. The interior of the villa felt suddenly quiet after the party; like a tomb. No sound was audible in the vast interior. Persian carpets, seemly laid haphazardly on the stone floor, slept as if exhausted by the foray of giant steps thudding into their delicate fabric. The massive dinning table, forlorn, a central area of demolished delicacies contained within an outer circle of high backed pseudo-Louis XV carver chairs, thrust back from the table edge at crazy angles as departing guests had forcefully levered their bottoms between tight-fitting armrests.

Sami could have sworn that during the general mass exit, the occasional sucking sound added lewd overtures to the rhapsody of farewells. Food remnants splattered the delicately decorated walls in a faint multi-coloured patina. Every now and then, the discolouration was disturbed by clean patches. Each clean area resembling some grotesque semi-human outline. Sami had already noticed a similar veneer on the bosoms of some guests. He had concluded that the rapidity of conversations and consumption of food had resulted in a vocal delivery of Arabic accompanied by physical punctuation in the form of food particles. It was akin to paint spraying, he thought to himself.

Barking instructions to his wife that the servants should clear away the mess, Sami made his way to the sanctity of his study. He remained there behind locked doors for the rest of the day, and well into the night. It was after midnight that he finally picked up the telephone and dialled a number. The ringing tone continued for some time. Eventually the receiver was lifted and a sleepy voice cautiously enquired, 'Ello. Nam.'

Sami, dispensing with the usual courtesies, gruffly instructed Omar (the waiter) to come over to the villa immediately. Sami had devised a plan of action. Omar was to implement it immediately. Omar's protestations fell on deaf ears. Sami had already replaced the receiver.

Samantha was in seventh heaven. She had seen Simon off at Heathrow Airport and, returning to her parked car, she literally fell over cascading baggage, hitting her head a glancing blow against the side of a rogue airport trolley. Giles Lawson, arriving from a rugby tour, had disembarked and had collected his personal luggage from the carousel in Terminal 3. His selection of trolleys was less than propitious, as it clearly had a strong disposition against heavy loads. It took every evasive action to shed its load throughout Giles' tortuous negotiations through customs, into arrivals and towards the short-term car park of Terminal 3. It was at the approach to the car park that the trolley, sensing his sudden lack of concentration, decided to deposit Giles' baggage directly in front of a passing young beauty. As the bags fell, one directly in Samantha's path, she tripped and toppled into the confusion. Giles, for an instant, felt acute embarrassment. He hesitated only for a moment before bending over the spread-eagled figure.

Giles was accustomed to rugby injuries and he correctly surmised that the adorable creature was only slightly stunned. He was well satisfied with the tirade of muted anger that followed her re-entry into full consciousness. He helped Samantha regain her feet and Samantha rapidly regained her composure. His apologies were profuse and sincere. It was agreed that he would escort her to the nearest airport restaurant to give her time to gather herself prior to her drive back to London. Samantha's initial reaction was one of hesitation. She was still angry, but realised that driving in an unsettled mental condition could slow her reactions in the fast motorway traffic. Giles chose a comfortable, corner table and ordered tea. Neither of them realised that their subsequent conversation would change their lives forever.

The following day was Christmas Day and Samantha had already made plans. On December 29th she was flying to Beirut to join her parents and Simon. Christmas Day and Boxing Day were fully occupied. The following days, prior to leaving for Beirut, would be a social round of parties. As they got to know each other and the relationship developed, Giles gently insisted that he should drive Samantha home.

He parked his BMW 535i outside Samantha's apartment, handed her the keys of the BMW and returned by Underground to Heathrow to collect Samantha's car. Samantha's office had already been notified of the incident and they had been adamant that she should visit her local GP for a brief examination. If she was well enough, she would be expected to attend the office party later that evening. Samantha busied herself in the solitude of the apartment tidying this and that. She decided she felt quite well. A visit to the nice Dr Williams didn't seem justified. Anyway it was such a fag.

The intercom to the outer entrance door buzzed. It was Giles announcing his return. Samantha released the electronic catch on the outer door. After a pause she heard his footsteps pounding up the staircase and he presented himself at the open door of the apartment, bearing in one hand a bunch of beautiful red roses.

Samantha had two passions in life, doughnuts and red roses. As she looked at the tall, elegant, handsome man framed in the door opening, she felt the faint stirrings of emotions, and the possibility of a third passion. The rest of the day they spent together. Samantha arrived at the office party. She was alone, she was late and she was preoccupied.

Christmas Day dawned. The apartment seemed strangely quiet. Samantha's flatmate was spending Christmas with her parents in Godalming, Surrey, and the tranquillity of London, after the general clamour of traffic and its frenzied activity, seemed alien. Halfway through a lonely breakfast, the outer door intercom buzzed impatiently. Giles had returned, bearing a profusion of red roses and some gift-wrapped presents. He apologized for arriving unexpectedly, but added that he felt responsible for Samantha's condition and needed reassurance as to her well-being. He had brought her a few things as a token of his sincerity.

'Whilst I'm delighted to see you, you could quite easily have telephoned,' Samantha said.

Giles regarded her with a twinkle in his eye. 'That wouldn't have satisfied me at all,' he replied, as he closed the apartment door behind him.

Within the hour, Samantha had telephoned her friends to cancel Christmas lunch, apologising that she felt unwell after the incident yesterday at the airport and would they forgive her. She reassured them that she would be in touch on her return from Beirut. Wishing them a very happy Christmas, she replaced the receiver and turned to Giles.

They had a hilarious day down on the South Coast, living it up at the Grand Hotel. During the following days they became inseparable, and it was with mixed emotions that she kissed Giles farewell at Heathrow Airport immediately prior to boarding the MEA flight to Beirut. On landing at Beirut International Airport, she experienced the same welcoming hospitality as Simon in crossing no-man's-land. Waiting for her in the arrivals lounge were her parents and Simon. The family was reunited. Giles telephoned later, to satisfy himself that she had arrived safely.

Ian had indigestion. The family Christmas had been demanding. Janette was still experiencing 'strange events'. She had related over Christmas lunch the latest episode of the continuing saga. She had had to visit the local chiropodist, Sole and Toe Co. Her bunions were again causing her trouble and she wanted treatment prior to Christmas. Whilst in the waiting room, reading *Country Life*, Mrs Wildes, who was rather fat and married to a chartered surveyor, was also waiting for an appointment. Her corns were causing her discomfort. Anyway, as soon as the receptionist left, presumably to visit the toilet, she sidled over to Janette, sat down on the adjoining chair and started to whisper.

'Do you know what she said?' Janette asked Ian.

'No, of course not, you weren't there. Well, she told me that her marriage to Harold, that's her husband, wasn't her first. In fact, he's her second. According to her, her first husband was an absolute rotter. Harold, her present husband, in comparison is a delight. Theobold, the first husband, I think that was his name, used to play golf. Harold doesn't play anything. He does the pools every week. Never won anything, of course, but he still keeps trying. Yes, sorry, I'm digressing. Theobold had a secret affair with the lady down at the dry cleaners. She said she could never understand, why after his golfing afternoons, he always returned wearing a clean shirt. Well, I ask you, she said, men playing sweaty games! You must admit it's a bit strange. It was his balls that gave him away. Of course, I was totally nonplussed at that. I asked her what 'balls' had to do with her discovering that her husband was having an affair? Do you know what she said? No, of course not, you weren't there. Well, she looked me straight in the eye and said, "Oh my dear, you are so innocent." With that she returned to her seat just as Mr Sole, the senior practitioner, called her in for her appointment. I was seeing Mr Toe, so I didn't get the opportunity to speak to her again.'

Ian felt his paper hat slipping. He had a sudden urge to go out into the fresh air and clean the car. Janette swivelled as young Alexander hit William. 'Don't do that to your younger brother, Alexander,' she said. 'I've told you before about bullying. It's not nice.'

'But Mum, he called me a cross-eyed toady creep,' Alexander replied.

The accusations and counter-accusations continued for the rest of the lunch, only decreasing after the second helping of Christmas pudding. By this time, Ian's indigestion had the added misery of wind. Ian made his escape to the kitchen where he added to the savoury smells of cooking.

★

Omar was cold. His wife and four of their children were asleep in the double bed, snugly cocooned in threadbare blankets. He stretched out tentatively, not wishing to disturb the slumbering quartet, to pluck a loose edge of the blanket whilst surreptitiously wriggling closer to the warm dormant bodies. The old mattress protested shrilly at the redistribution of weight. His wife, subconsciously uneasy at the sudden noise, twisted tighter into her foetal position, tearing away from Omar's clutching fingers the last vestige of covering. He lay there, shivering in the morning chill, a pathetic figure, starkly illuminated by nearby road lamps, shining through the dirty window.

The following day, Boxing Day, was a traditional European Holiday. The origins of Boxing Day are obscured in the mists of time. It was when the families opened their presents. It also enabled recuperation from the previous day's excesses. Modern society had abandoned the ritual of delaying present opening, although the facility to recuperate remained much in evidence. The Moslem societies have no comparable day and the commercial activities of Beirut were semi-functional.

Felicity had, early on Boxing Day morning, telephoned Samantha for their usual 'girly' chat and to finalise plans for Samantha's skiing holiday. Her visit would overlap Simon by a couple of days causing great excitement in the household. Prior to concluding the conversation, Felicity had requested that Samantha purchase a quantity of a specific brand of confectionary in London. Samantha mused, as she replaced the receiver, whether her mother was pregnant, as the quantity requested was enormous.

Simon had contacted Victor Walpole. He had reassured him that he was safely ensconced in Beirut and he saw no problem in attending the scheduled meetings previously arranged by Victor. Before concluding the conversation, Simon had asked Victor to contact Ian McEwan and Thomas Norman St John. Each of them was required to make a special purchase in London prior to their visit. Victor faithfully passed on the message, musing as he did so that one was surprised at the amount of the specified article.

Chapter 7

The Lebanese civil war had all but destroyed the Beirut Central District, the heart and soul of Lebanon. Pre-1974, Lebanon had enjoyed an enviable reputation as a cultural and financial centre for the Middle East. It was the playground for many wealthy tourists, and the crowded streets heaved with a multitude of different nationalities, each one seeking to satisfy his own personal needs in the cosmopolitan community. International businessmen, actively seeking wealth-creating opportunities from the emerging oil-rich Middle Eastern countries, would travel to Beirut, with the knowledge that a Lebanese business partner was their passport to future success. Beirut, located as it was at the crossroads of East and West, heavily trafficked by travellers passing through, proved a fertile breeding ground for exchanging reliable information on Middle Eastern intrigues that could influence future Western Government policies. Beirut was a favoured place for diplomats and spies. The ill-clad, long-haired new world traveller, backpack on back, would visit Beirut to vanish into the Bekaa valley, only to reappear after the novelty of coupling with nature's resources had run its course and destiny decreed another onward journey. Retired businessmen and their long-suffering wives, weary of civilisation in the first world, would tend their raspberry gardens, secluded in the mountains surrounding Beirut, as they struggled to come to grips with the Arabic language and a new home. Beirut International Airport was alive twenty-four hours a day. Passengers would disembark from East and West, North and South, to join the jostling melee thronging the capital of Lebanon, Beirut. Beirut offered something for everybody. It was an international playground.

The seasons would see snow covered mountains in winter dotted with youthful skiers, who, adorned in their warm ski suits, collectively represented the colours of the rainbow starkly highlighted by the virgin whiteness of the snow. The fertile lower slopes, fed with a network of crystal clear springs, supported the abundant orchards that over the coming months would fill the market stalls with succulent fruit of every variety. Mountain walkers, gathering in the red-roofed mountain villages, would begin their treks into the craggy hinterland in the knowledge that they would see history, the hermit holes, churches and monasteries, built into the vertical rock face, home to devout beings, dedicated to meditation and worship. As they began their journey across the uncompromising mountainous terrain, they could smell history, strong in their nostrils. The golden sand covering the glorious beaches, crowded with lithe bronze bodies screaming with excitement as the clear Mediterranean waters cooled the perspiring bodies, already tanning under the warmth of the benevolent rays of the sun. These activities all happening under the constant faultless blue of the sky above. This was surely a land that God had blessed.

Beirut boasted many universities, the predominant being the American University of Beirut. The university had been founded in the nineteenth century and was an established seat of learning. It was located to the north of Beirut City in a campus that many considered the most attractive in the world. Beirut was a Mecca for many learned academics, attracting students from all over the globe. With this wealth of culture, the learned professions proliferated, and the capital was rich in human resources. The Lebanese, following in the footsteps of their Phoenician forefathers, traded extensively in these resources, making great contributions to the development of the emerging oil-rich countries that were their neighbours. Money, consequently, flowed into Lebanon.

The natural disposition of the Lebanese as a fun-loving people gave impetus to the many social activities available throughout the capital. Restaurants, filled to capacity, would see a procession of waiters serving delicious Lebanese food well into the early hours as the revellers, drawing on an inexhaustible supply of energy, danced and cavorted until dawn. Hotels, storehouses of oriental artefacts, offered their guests delights undreamed of, and the hotel pools provided early morning solitude and recovery after the previous night's enjoyment. Fashion shows, gambling and entertainment from a galaxy of international stars all made their contribution to the reputation of this wonderful city that never slept. The more seedy aspects of Beirut, albeit a shadowy parallel to the published activities, heaved and grunted under the extraordinary demand for the luscious ladies parading in and out of the red-light areas.

Commerce thrived with unbelievable activity. Enlivened by bitter Arabic coffee, haggling would continue for hours. Be it only in the purchase of a Persian carpet, some gold trinkets, a business venture or the purchase of a seemingly insignificant article, the joy of business was in the negotiations. The country responded with a zest that only the multi-talented and multilingual population of Lebanon possessed.

Palestinian refugee camps pulsated with the forlorn hope of a forgotten people. The inequity of total poverty against prosperity fuelled resentment at an accelerating rate. In 1974, an isolated event gave the country reason to pause. However, it continued to ignore the cancerous situation developing.

In May 1994, a private development company was formed. Its purpose: the reconstruction of Beirut Central District. The area acquired for redevelopment extended to 455 acres of land upon which remained the monuments of man's futility in the art of destruction. Empty eye-socket buildings, pock-scarred with bullet holes, blindly stared at each other. Once proud buildings, now lumps of rubble, conveyed desolation, despair and despondency to a nation reeling with suffering. The civil war had ceased in 1989. As the nation licked its wounds, bewildered by events over the last couple of decades, it wondered how the patient could ever recover and how to begin the period of recuperation.

Disaster sometimes creates the seed of its own salvation. An eminently successful Lebanese businessman, returning to Beirut after a prolonged period abroad, possessed sufficient vision and courage to view the devastation as a business opportunity. He formed a development company called Solidere. As the years rolled passed the gradual reconstruction of Beirut Central District brought symbolic hope to a united country. It became a symbol of the re-emergence from that dark period. Beautiful buildings slowly emerged from the rubbish tips. People gathered confidence as the new buildings slowly forced destruction and despair into the inner recesses of the mind. Multi-storey buildings clad in gleaming marble, glistening glass or soft beige limestone, softened the barren landscape. Restaurants began to open, few at first, and gradually the people raised their heads in wonder as the new Beirut took on an identity of national focus. The redevelopment began to transform the nation, but the task was Herculean and not without political problems as the politicians bickered amongst themselves.

Angus Sharples, town planner to Solidere, wiped his perspiring brow with the back of his hand, then as he absently picked his nose, the telephone rang. Angus was preoccupied. The original master plan had undergone considerable modification since its conception. With an area of redevelopment, approximately three-quarters the size of the City of London, he reconciled his frustrations with the magnitude of the project. The latest modification entailed the introduction of a Grand Prix racetrack and he was currently examining the best route through the labyrinth of roads and boulevards that criss-crossed the area. Initially, he had listened with incredulity as his director discussed it with him. They are mad, he thought to himself. The everyday driving had honed his skills at accident avoidance to a fine edge. He dreaded the thought of providing further facilities for the Lebanese Mad Max types to prove their manhood and the unreliability of their ancient vehicles through his beloved development. It would destroy the tranquillity of the area. It wasn't as if there weren't sufficient go-cart racing circuits in the area. His director reassured him that the Grand Prix racetrack was for the Beirut Grand Prix, planned to commence in 2005. Unofficial stock car racing would not be allowed, and the proposal had been endorsed by the President. Once reassured, Angus had devoted all of his energies to incorporating the proposals into the development, as he could clearly see the Beirut Grand Prix as a potential money-spinner.

The voice at the other end of the telephone brought him out of his reflections. He was unable to identify the caller due to line interference and asked, 'Who's speaking?' Immediately on hearing the retort, 'You are,' he knew it was Wajid Chehayed, Solidere's chief project manager. Wajid was a talented middle-aged Lebanese engineer, educated in the West. He had been born with a sense of humour, and constantly regaled his friends and associates with jokes and anecdotes. Angus relaxed in the comfort of his high-backed office chair in the knowledge that the conversation would take some time as Wajid reeled off a couple of jokes as a prelude to the purpose of his telephone call. Eventually, as the laughter petered out, Wajid came to the point.

'Angus, my friend, you know that in the master construction program, Buildings 120 to 122 are scheduled to start next month. Well, I just want to confirm that all is ready to go. We expect starting the works within the next four weeks. Do you know if the building permits have been granted, and are the contracts signed with the contractors?'

Angus delved deep into his mind. 'Yes, I'm pretty certain that the permits have been issued by the municipality but I'll check with the legal department. I'm also sure that the work will be organised in work packages. We intend using our own people for the restoration of the stonework. We still have to finalise negotiations on the electro-mechanical elements. As you know, this will follow the restoration of the external façade. In principle, I cannot foresee that you should have problems in starting the works as planned. Why don't you check with the architects that their drawings and specifications are all finished?'

Angus listened to another couple of jokes from Wajid, as a farewell encore, prior to replacing the receiver on its cradle at the same time as the man at the other end. He returned to his problem of including a racetrack into the grand scheme.

Omar stopped the wheezing Vespa motor scooter and surveyed his surroundings. He had earlier that morning borrowed the battered machine from his brother-in-law, and despite its dilapidated condition, it had propelled him in fits and starts from Hamra Street to Beirut Central District. Omar felt exposed on the tiny scooter but reasoned that it afforded him mobility. The law of the jungle, in circumventing one-way streets, could be relatively safely adopted by weaving in and out of the oncoming traffic; the irate tooting of horns, at his unpredictable passing, was a cross to bear. Stationary, he sat, straddling the tiny seat as he unrolled the drawing clutched in his sweating hand. It was a large layout plan of the Beirut Central District, delineating individual plots, and it had been 'borrowed' by Sami from the Town Planning Department. The roll continued to unravel, and soon Omar's arms, extended to their full extent began to tire. The drawing was A.1 metric standard size (150 x 90cm). To oncoming traffic, he resembled a low, mounted, blank billboard.

In some warm climates, it is the local custom to extend arms out of vehicle windows. The custom originated after the discovery of the beneficial cooling action on perspiring bodies. It was not an uncommon sight to see old service taxis sprouting an assortment of hairy appendages. Beirut contained many of these gigantic hybrid spiders, the rusty mechanical body waving its multitude of hairy arms. Unknown to Omar, one such vehicle was approaching his blind side. He sat, straddled on the tiny seat, studiously studying the unfurled drawing, when suddenly the drawing was whipped away from his fingers. He flailed his hands to regain possession of the paper but it was too late, the service taxi had passed. He turned in disbelief as the rear of the dilapidated Mercedes sped by, belching clouds of dark exhaust fumes into his open mouth. There, protruding from the passenger window was an outstretched arm. Wrapped around the arm was a large sheet of paper. He heard laughter as the vehicle passed. Hurling curses, Omar gunned the scooter into life. It fired once, twice and then died. Omar watched in panic as the taxi receded into the distance, the flapping paper waving goodbye. He stood, dejected and forlorn, wondering what to do. He was afraid to return to Sami with yet another excuse.

Abandoning the useless scooter, Omar began to walk aimlessly towards the new part of Beirut Central District. Shuffling through the labyrinth of deserted streets, he contemplated his situation with despair. His family were growing up and making increasing demands. Sami's contribution to the household expenditure was meagre; it was barely sufficient to put food on the table. Omar's evening job as a waiter paid the rent and it was only the handouts from his cousin in America that clothed the family. His wife's uncle, ever complaining, contributed towards school fees; but at the end of the day, Omar had no money left to pay for utilities. He had an unofficial arrangement with some of the middle management of the utility companies, that in return for running errands, they would mislay his file for a couple of months. Omar contemplated his hand-to-mouth existence with desperation, conscious that Sami's patience with Omar's bungling was almost at an end.

Oblivious to his surroundings, he had arrived at the Foch-Allenby area. The new City Centre had been restored with Martyrs Square as its core. The new development formed concentric rings, Radiating outwards like annual tree rings of gigantic dimensions. Broad avenues of pedestrian walkways bisected tall newly renovated sandstone-clad buildings, each embellished with magnificent masonry ornamentations. Many of the buildings had been built in the French colonial style with tall, shuttered windows, cantilevered balconies and ornate wrought iron balustrades. Their subsequent renovation had brought out the beauty of the original design. Here and there, eastern mosques with domed roofs covered with decorative tiling, their slender minarets peeping over adjacent parapet levels, complemented the European churches with their multi-level red-tiled roofs and majestic façades. The whole area had a tranquillity that was only disturbed by the raucous din of distant compressors, hammering away in the bowels of some building not yet completed. The Foch-Allenby area was generally designated a commercial area. On ground floors, shopfronts looked for retail tenants whilst the upper floors served as offices. The buildings were gradually filling up as tenants moved in, and as Omar walked, he passed, scattered amongst the empty shops, windows displaying ladies fashions with tasteful displays, art galleries, antique shops, cafes, small family run restaurants and the like, that any modern city provides for its population. By chance, Omar paused outside a real estate shop window and happened to glance in. There, spread out on a massive table, was a model of the whole development. He looked closer. He saw that whilst making the model, the model maker had used a chart similar to the one that Sami had 'borrowed' –

albeit on a far larger scale. Each plot had a design number, and whilst tiny buildings had been superimposed in the plot, in the majority of cases, the plot designation was clearly visible. He looked around the well-lit walls of the shop searching for something else that would provide the information he needed. The walls were decorated with a display of residential units for sale. Nothing else that was meaningful caught Omar's eye but he was reassured that all was not lost. He retraced his steps to the abandoned scooter and now there was a spring in his walk.

John scanned the *Daily Star* over breakfast the following day. An article caught his eye. There had been a break-in in the Foch-Allenby area. Little damage had been caused, as only the entrance door lock had been forced, but the police were mystified. A model of Beirut Central District had been stolen. John mused as he munched his way through the meal. Who on earth would steal a model of Beirut Central District that measured 10 feet x 15 feet? he thought to himself. He put it down to some Syrian worker who, returning home to Damascus, wanted a doll's house for his young children. He then dismissed it from his mind.

Omar, reinvigorated with the success of the previous night's sortie was relatively happy. He had telephoned Sami to provide the daily update on the results of his investigation. Sami had grunted a reply, indirectly congratulating him. Secreted in Omar's bedroom was the stolen model. It had caused problems with the family sleeping arrangements but Omar had arranged that six of his children would stay with other members of his extended family during the investigation. He explained to his long-suffering brother-in-law that the scooter had been dowsed with waste by a sewage collecting tanker during its discharge of septic tank effluent into the Beirut mains sewage waste system. The hose coupling had burst, just as Omar was passing. Omar, in possession of the model, began to make further notes.

Sami had reasoned that Omar (the detective) had received information that was sufficient to locate the missing cache. All he had to do was to follow the line of reasoning that Omar (the detective) had followed. He resumed his study of the torn exercise book. For reasons that he could not explain, he felt confident that his search was at last on the right lines. He must make sure that Omar followed his instructions to the letter.

The following day, Felicity and the children decided to venture onto the ski slopes at Faraya. John had left early to face a full day's work at the office. The run-up to Faraya was relatively uneventful. Felicity felt safe driving the 4 x 4 Grand Cherokee as the vehicle was so sturdy that the occasional 'crunch' signifying minor impacts from passing miss-directed cars did not prove any impediment to the continuous ebb and flow of family conversation. Approaching the snow-capped mountains of Lebanon was truly awe-inspiring. The blue Mediterranean Sea gradually receded as the magnificent white peaks became more prominent until they filled the windscreen. Felicity already owned her ski equipment but it was necessary to kit out the two children. Stopping at Val d' Isère, one of the many ski hire equipment shops, dotted below the approach to Faraya, she left Samantha and Simon to the tender care of Roni Khalil whilst she popped next door to procure a traditional Arabic breakfast of *Manouchi* washed down with Arabic coffee. Roni fussed around the children like a mother hen, and eventually, both Samantha and Simon emerged clutching the necessary equipment. The family grouped outside Roni's, as they munched their breakfast. Roni, in broken English, told them about the snow conditions and the best slopes. Thus fortified, with knowledge and sustenance, they drove the last couple of kilometres to Faraya Mzar, where Felicity parked the Cherokee in the already bustling car park. The Lebanese winter is both aggressive and kind. Violent electric storms deposit vast quantities of snow at the higher altitudes; at lower altitudes, it is torrential rain. Balmy days provide playtime intervals and the snow-covered slopes now glistened in the winter sunshine. The weather was gorgeous. Felicity rapidly changed into her ski boots and hobbled off in the direction of the ticket office. Samantha and Simon followed at a more leisurely pace, skis draped very professionally over their shoulders, treading carefully with exaggerated steps on the compacted snow. The vista opened up and they espied the numerous chairlifts mechanically growling and hissing as they whisked chatting and laughing skiers up into the beyond. For hours they forgot the world as they all gave themselves up to the delights and challenges of skiing in the wintry wilderness.

John's day had proved less than enjoyable. He was frustrated. He was continuously being assigned assistants whom he rigorously trained. Once they received a level of professional competence that would relieve him of some of his more menial tasks, they would suddenly be reassigned and he would have to repeat the process of training all over again. They were, he contemplated, like rabbits popping out of a magician's top hat only to vanish again at the end of their performance. His current assistant, Rola Itani, was a Lebanese flower in full bloom. Her intellectual capabilities had impressed John and over a short period a relationship had developed. That morning he had been informed that Rola was to be assigned to the office in Dubai. She was to be replaced by Najib Chika. John knew of Najib by reputation: a hyperactive chatterbox, suffering from an inflated opinion of his capabilities, which when pressed, tended to burst into a torrent of excuses. To make matters worse, Najib had received a full French education. John's depression deepened, as he subconsciously compared the exiting beauty against the incoming beast. Contributing to his depression was the looming target date for the renovation of the building containing the cache of gold. It was becoming increasingly urgent that he implemented his plan of action, the principles of which had been discussed at the family gathering over Christmas Day.

It was all very well, he thought to himself, sitting in this palatial office, shuffling pieces of paper around, when the opportunity existed to benefit the youngsters of Lebanon and it was out there waiting. The problem was, he mused to himself, how to smuggle the bullion away from the building site, under the noses of the watchful guards. He was aware that Solidere having experienced a period of pilfering (a couple of JCBs had vanished, together with various Roman artefacts and other articles of value to the enterprising Lebanese), was very much on its guard. Firm instructions to the armed security guards had been issued that nothing was to be moved from any site without express written orders from the Ministry of Planning and Development, separately verified by Solidere and presented by a minor official from the Ministry and a known director of Solidere. John began to marshal his thoughts as his intellect focused on the problem. Behind him sat Rola, dabbing the tears from her eyes, saddened by the news of her pending departure. During the course of the morning, John made a couple of telephone calls unconnected with work. Unknown to John, Rola had visited the personnel department.

★

Over the course of the next few days, both Ian McEwan and Thomas Norman St John arrived in Beirut. Ian, barely able to contain his excitement, exited Beirut International Arrivals dressed in a charcoal grey business suit, black brogues and silk tie and wearing a Bensons handmade shirt. He looked very much the smart executive. On his head was a scarlet fez. Janette had remonstrated at Heathrow Airport but Ian was adamant that he should blend into the community and do as the Romans do. Janette nonplussed at first but rapidly gathering her wits, retorted, 'What do you mean? The Romans live in Rome. I thought you were going to Beirut!'

Ian brushed this cutting remark aside. 'You know what I mean,' he replied, and with a dry kiss placed on her proffered cheek, about-turned. Janette watched her husband's diminishing back as he jauntily approached passport control, scarlet fez bobbing in the distance, and vanished from view.

Janette bit her lip. The 'happenings' were still bothering her. She had refrained from telling Ian about the latest event due to his preoccupation with this business trip. The memory welled up in her mind as she recalled it. She had stopped at some red traffic lights where she had been approached by a policeman. The officer had asked for her name and address, and these she meekly provided. On her asking about her offence, the officer had just laughed and explained they were having a sweepstake down at the station. With that he walked away, leaving Janette agog – and for once speechless.

Thomas Norman St John, dressed in a black full-length overcoat with black sombrero pulled down over his eyes, departed from Heathrow Airport without undue attention. He arrived at Beirut International Airport, exited Arrivals and mingled easily with the milling crowd. Ian had preceded Thomas by a full day. They met up at the coffee shop in the Phoenicia Hotel. Immediately prior to this meeting, Ian had telephoned Simon at his parents' apartment to announce his safe arrival, and it was arranged that they would all dine together that night. The invitation included John, Felicity and Samantha. They dined at the Istanbullie, sampling typical Lebanese food, washed down with arack. The waiter asked, as Ian entered the restaurant, preceded by Felicity and Samantha, whether he wished to leave his fez at the check-in. During the course of the meal it was agreed that Thomas, Ian and Simon would have a business meeting the following day with Kamal Bsat's lawyers, about the St George Hotel. The fez gradually slid forward over Ian's eyes as the level in the arack bottle dropped. Only his ears, now angled and protruding at 180 degrees from his head, acted as retaining stops to the felt covering over his thinning hair. During the course of the evening, both Ian and Thomas handed packages procured in London over to John.

Chapter 8

Closeted in Sami's study, Omar fidgeted nervously. He stood facing Sami, who was seated behind the broad expanse of a well-worn and battered desk. The top of the desk was littered with scraps of paper, discarded cigar wrappings and a homogenous noxious mass of unidentifiable material. A faint odour, wafted gently around the room. In one corner, reverently cleared of the adjacent litter, lay the old exercise book.

'Show me!' shouted Sami. The ensuing pause caused him to glance up. He saw Omar seemingly struggling with some invisible opponent. His chest heaved and twisted. Unknown to him, Omar had fidgeted his fingers into a locked intertwine and he was unable to disengage them. With a slight thwack from behind Omar's back, his arms suddenly freed themselves, and from shoulder height a podgy finger zoomed down and speared a scrap of paper, that lay haphazardly on top of the desk. Sami stared at the crumpled sheet.

'Yes,' he said to himself. 'Yes, that's possible.' Quick as a flash he seized it, stuffed it into a half-open drawer and slammed the drawer shut.

Over the weeks Sami had ridden Omar hard. Ignoring Omar's snivels and pleas, Sami was relatively pleased with the results so far accomplished. He had identified three possible buildings that corresponded generally with the fragmented information contained in the old exercise book. He had not confided in Omar and on purpose Omar had been sent out on many false trails. That this had extended the time, Sami regretted, but he felt it was necessary and it gave him comfort in the knowledge that he alone was collecting the information. There was one last area requiring investigation. Sami rapidly barked instructions at Omar. He waited whilst Omar repeated them, and once word-perfect, told him to get out and come back in forty-eight hours with results. He watched the back of the forlorn figure as it shuffled towards the study door. The slam of the outer door heralded Omar's departure. Sami sat in the solitude of his untidy study contemplating his next step. The faint odour seemed less pungent.

Sami instinctively knew that his quest would soon be over. But how to remove the bullion from under the noses of the guards? He mentally juggled with various options. Three emerged. (1) Unofficial midnight visit. (2) Bribing the security officer or (3) Why not be legitimate, and tender for the works? He discarded (1): the site was too closely watched. A midnight visit would entail a vehicle and Omar and others. It was too conspicuous. (2) He had already done his fair share of bribing. His construction company had benefited hugely from 'redundant' Solidere site equipment and the Roman artefacts had fetched a good price in Dubai. (3) He reasoned that tendering for the works would give him legitimate reasons to visit the buildings. He would be authorised to move construction equipment and materials in and out of the area without restrictions, other than a cursory inspection, and without creating any suspicion. A thought crossed his mind that he would also be contributing to the future of his country, but this emotion was fleeting as it was rapidly replaced by his mental calculations on the profit the project could generate if he pitched his tender price correctly.

Once he'd decided that Option 3 was the only viable one, Sami picked up the telephone and called Solidere to enquire about their future tender packages programmes. It was agreed that the list would be sent around to Sami by courier that afternoon. Later that night, Sami studied the list of future projects from Solidere. The schedule contained two lists. One related to demolition and reconstruction; the other to the renovation of existing buildings. By a process of elimination, Sami identified one of the buildings scheduled as one appearing in his list. Package 45.3 included the demolition and reconstruction of Building 80.1. He made a note in his work diary. He would formally request tender documents for package 45.3 tomorrow. By greasing a few palms he knew he would be awarded the project.

The offices of Kamal Bsat's lawyer were situated on the tenth floor of a high-rise tower building in the Manara area of Beirut. Its orientation provided magnificent views of the Mediterranean Sea on two sides, whilst the third and fourth sides were crowded in between original low-rise Lebanese mansions with their large red-tiled pitched roofs and ancient verandas, jostling for space with the new high-rise luxury apartments, all erected without consideration as to density. Parked cars littered the street, abandoned at crazy angles, almost precluding the free passage of passing vehicles. Thomas and Simon had considerable difficulty in locating the building, due to Ian's atrocious pronunciation of Arabic. Eventually, and after numerous telephone calls from the driver's mobile, they received directions and were deposited at the entrance.

Entering the building, Simon remarked, 'Wonder when this was last cleaned.' The place looked musty and felt tired. He surveyed the chipped marble walls and floors as Ian located the lawyer's office, displayed in the faded wall-mounted office location board. The mounting had corroded over the years, and it had slipped to one side. 'Ah, yes,' Ian said, 'he's on the tenth floor.'

Thomas had already called the elevator. They squeezed into the tiny cabin. Gradually they ascended the building with squeaks and squeals of protesting mechanical parts until they reached the tenth floor. The elevator doors opened onto a narrow dingy corridor. Office doors were located at either end. Sign-writing on the glazed panel of the door to the extreme left proclaimed that that was the offices of Dr Aboud-Enien and Associates.

The reception area was extremely bright in contrast to the common circulation parts. The area was light and clean. Pictures adorned the walls and here and there the area was dotted with potted plants. It had an air of enjoyable activity. A face appeared above the top of a low partition screen, and with a musical voice, tinkling with amusement, asked if she could be of assistance to them. Ian cleared his throat as he looked full face into a beautiful woman. He stuttered the introductions, concluding that they had an appointment with Dr Aboud-Enien, There emerged from behind the screen a magnificent creature, who quickly turned only to vanish in the labyrinth of corridors Radiating from the main reception.

Simon turned to Thomas. 'How do they produce so many gorgeous women?' he said. Thomas mumbled a reply that he was too old for that sort of thing but he admitted that the proportion of beautiful creatures was certainly extremely high. He could make use of those curves in some of his new designs.

The magnificent creature returned. She beckoned them to follow as she led them into the inner sanctum of the office. Simon couldn't take his eyes off her undulating posterior as they marched down the corridor noting many delightful secretaries on his way. The feminine chatter subsided as Simon passed, as similar thoughts ran through each mind. Standing at an open door was a small runt of a man. He was wearing a threadbare three-piece suit, fob-watch chain dangling across his lower chest, and his eyes, through half-moon glasses, danced with intelligence as he greeted them and ushered them all into his inner office. The office was light and airy. On two half-sides, book-lined shelving extended from floor to ceiling. The other halves and the third side contained full height panoramic windows with extensive views of the sea.

Introductions were made as another beautiful young creature appeared bearing a silver tray containing tiny cups of the traditional Arabic coffee. She dispensed these efficiently but lingered around Simon. As her long blond hair brushed his shoulder he caught a glimpse of beautiful green eyes set in a perfect face – and as she departed, the smell of an expensive French perfume lingered.

Dr Aboud-Enien had already commenced with an update on the situation. Ian had previously contacted the Lebanese Embassy in London and they had assured him that if Mr Kamal Bsat provided firm evidence that he fully intended to renovate his property, the St George Hotel, and if international investors were fully committed to funding the project, the Embassy had no reason to doubt that the Government of Lebanon would not exercise their option of confiscation. The Government's policy was the reconstruction of Beirut and they needed the confidence and money of foreign investment. The meeting progressed, notwithstanding being constantly interrupted by the ringing of various telephones arranged along Dr Aboud-Enien's desk. Dr Aboud-Enien apologised and explained that an urgent constitutional matter had occurred the previous day. He felt unable to cancel the meeting as it was urgent but he hoped that Mr Ian, Mr Simon and Mr Thomas would understand and accept these irritating telephone calls. They were of national importance. Ian was amazed at Dr Aboud-Enien's ability to rapidly switch from fluent English to Arabic and French in the course of a single conversation. Replacing the receiver after another multilingual exchange, Dr Aboud-Enien summed up.

'Well, gentlemen, we have now discussed the general situation quite fully. Perhaps I can put it in a nutshell so there is no room for any misunderstanding. The elected Government are fully entitled, under the provisions of Decree No 19438, to serve notice of their intent to confiscate Mr Bsat's property. He has made no effort to comply with the law and as such must suffer the consequences. However, after representation from your company, Mr Ian, through our Embassy in London, the Government is prepared to delay the issue of this Notice of Intent under certain conditions. I believe that our Embassy have already conveyed this decision to you. However, the Government feel that they are entitled to consideration in that respect. It is accepted that this was not conveyed to you by our Embassy officials. You will appreciate, that this is a delicate matter, which should be regarded as unofficial. The official conditions are (I) Mr Bsat must demonstrate that he is prepared to commence the renovation works to the St George Hotel and a contractor must be appointed and active in these renovation works within the next three months. (2) Mr Bsat must provide full details of the intended works, including evidence that he has all the necessary financial backing to complete the works.'

Thomas nodded to himself and Dr Aboud-Enien continued, 'Original documents purporting to support all of this information must be lodged with the Director of the Council of Development and Reconstruction (CDR) before midnight, on the 31st January. Failure to comply fully with this request will give the Government no other choice but to exercise their option on the relevant date and confiscate the property without compensation.

(3) As I have previously mentioned, the elected Government has made a concession to Mr Bsat. They feel that they are entitled to some consideration, The sum of $500,000 shall be paid into a special bank account to be nominated, and it shall be paid prior to close of business on 31st January. (4) Included in the list of Tenderers, two local contractors need to be nominated; and finally (5) once the Hotel is completed, special concessionary prices will be available to selected members of the elected Government for their unrestricted use of the Hotel. This facility shall be for a period of five years after the opening of the Hotel. I believe all these details are already included in the Arabic script already handed to you. For delicacy, conditions (3) and (5) are not included but, nevertheless, they shall apply. If all of these conditions are acceptable to Mr Bsat then, and only then, does he have a stay of execution. Any non-compliance, no matter how small, will nullify the arrangement and the elected Government will take possession on the prescribed date. I hope that is quite clear.'

The end of his recital coincided with the ringing of one of the telephones. Dr Aboud-Enien answered. 'Excuse me, Gentlemen. I am summoned to give an opinion in an adjacent office. One of my partners is currently talking with the President. I shall return in a few moments. You may ask of my staff anything you want during my absence.' The little man then rapidly exited the office.

Thomas was first to break the silence. 'Considering the amount of design work already done, so long as we adopt a fast-track design package, I believe that having a contractor on site within three months is just about possible. It will be very tight, but my staff usually work around the clock, so I don't see why this project should be any different. What about the rest of the conditions?' Ian looked at Simon, who was studying his shoelaces. 'Well, I don't know. We were not aware about this consideration thing at all. It all seemed so straightforward in London. We asked the question, and although there was a bit of 'humming and haaring', the answer came back without this consideration being raised. Yes, in principle, no problem. I suppose I must converse with our client, Kamal Bsat. What do you think, Simon?'

Simon had been distracted. The young lady had returned with another tray of Arabic coffee and some sweetmeats. She again lingered around Simon. 'Ah, yes Ian, quite so,' Simon replied, suddenly aware that both Ian and Thomas were staring at him. The young lady had casually brushed her hand against his. It was so soft and succulent. *God*, thought Simon to himself, *those eyes...*

Ian, thoughts focused on Janette, mentally 'eeny, meeny, miny, mo'd' the selection of telephones, and picked up the green one. He dialled Kamal Bsat's number.

Kamal was enjoying being back in Beirut. He could never understand the attractions of London or Paris. Beirut had it all. The previous night he had danced till dawn. His clarity of mind, never sparkling, was dull and sluggish this morning. He lifted the ringing receiver and with listless fingers, allowed it to drop back onto its cradle. After a pause, the phone rang again.

'*Marhaba*,' he said [Arabic for 'Hello'].'Oh yes, Ian... What do you want?... Do you know what time it is? Is it already! Well okay, What is it?... *You cannot be serious!* ★★★*! Well, negotiate! That's what I'm paying you guys for!*

With that he slammed the phone down. Kamal turned over to the slender nymph languishing beside him. '*Ta la horn*, my beauty,' he murmured, and immediately forgot about his conversation with Ian as he gave himself up to better things.

The meeting was concluded over lunch. It had been agreed with Mr Bsat, (providing various bedroom grunts), that the 'consideration' would be $350,000 paid in two equal instalments, one half due on the required date, the other half due once construction works had started. The special facilities would be made available for a period of three years to no more than four persons and 'unrestricted use' was rephrased to 'generous use'.

Ian felt quite drained as he removed his fez in the privacy of his hotel bedroom. He could hear Thomas, in the adjacent room, opening and closing the mini bar. Simon, however, was loitering around the lawyer's foyer, waiting for the green-eyed beauty.

The next day was busy. Ian briefed Victor Walpole about the meeting with Dr Aboud-Enien. It was agreed that Ian would return post haste to London accompanied by Simon. Nestling snugly in Ian's briefcase were all the necessary signed documents.

Thomas followed a couple of days later after finalising a sub-consultancy agreement with a Lebanese architectural practice. He reclined in his Club Class seat as the Middle East Airways airbus levelled out at 35,000 feet over Cyprus, and relaxed.

★

Smoke-laden, the sullen atmosphere whirled around the ceiling-mounted pinhole lights. Wall-mounted ornaments shuddered at the fluctuating impact of the deafening music. The hissing of the beer pumps made little contribution to the general melee of sound, which invaded every nook and cranny of the pub. It was Friday night, *Happy Hour*, when all the expats congregated together, reinvigorated by copious quantities of excellent draft Almaza beer, relaxing after the trials and tribulations of the working week. The Duke of Wellington had long been a favourite haunt of the expatriate community, Even during the war years, the crescendo of noise would almost deaden the crump of falling shells and obliterate the rat-tat-tat of machine-gun fire exchanged between deadly foes in the immediate vicinity, whilst the revellers, secluded in their cocoon of alcohol and companionship, exchanged pub jokes, gossiped or just larked around, secure in their belief that the Duke of Wellington was neutral ground.

Secluded in one corner, huddled around a low table, the profile of three hunched backs, curving upwards as if into a hairy bulbous cone, sat John and the two Mikes. They were in conference. As if tired by the cramped position, one of the backs, straightened, leant back, and swivelled his head in the general direction of the bar. Vision was limited due to the mass of wriggling bottoms, opening and closing ranks as the press of humanity gyrated as the need took them.

Mike Fleming was looking for a particularly shapely bottom. He had watched the owner as she had entered the pub with friends some time previously. He stood up, running his fingers through his blond hair. 'I say, you lot, what about another round? It's my shout, I believe.' Without waiting for a reply, Mike turned and threaded his way through the swaying assembly, generally in the direction of the bar but on a detour via the shapely bottom he had just espied.

Mike Brady regarded John with stern eyes. 'You know what will happen if we're nabbed,' he exclaimed.

John took another sip from his beer. 'It's not the Government that we should be unduly concerned about. All they will do is throw us in prison. The Embassy will get us out and we'll be deported. No big deal! It's the lawless elements that concern me. They'd have no compunction in dropping our corpses into the harbour.'

'Man,' exclaimed Mike. The conversation continued in muted tones as the beer levels descended to the bottom of the respective glasses.

Mike Fleming had targeted the shapely bottom rather well, he thought. Bumping into her, he had apologised profusely, introduced himself and soon they were in animated conversation. Halfway through a recital of one of Mike's favourite jokes, he felt the pressure of an enormous hand on his arm.

'What about our pints?' breathed a Northern Irish voice into Mike's ear.

'Oh, sod you, Mike Brady, you've just spoilt my joke! Oh, by the way, this is Joumana. Joumana, let me introduce you to Mike Brady. Over there, can you see, huddled in the corner? Yes, by the suit of armour, that's Johnny Meakin. Tell you what, Mike, let me finish this joke I'm telling Joumana, then I'll go get the beers. Joumana, I'm sure you would like a drink as well…'

Mike Brady regarded his friend Mike Fleming with a certain amount of pity. Anything wearing a skirt would set Mike off. Once focused, Mike would go the full distance. 'Tell you what, Mike,' he said, 'I'll get the drinks, John is gasping! We're just about finished anyway. Thought we'd join you and Joumana.'

Mike forced a grin, irritated that his friends were going to deprive him of his new playmate. 'Yes, well, that's alright with me. What about you, Joumana? Do you want these two old buggers to spoil the intimacy of our evening?'

Joumana smiled, wise as an owl, and with lilting voice, like a harp in heaven, she exclaimed, 'Perhaps you would all like to join me and *my* friends?'

The friends turned out to be a couple of young, rather tough-looking Lebanese engineers accompanied by their wives – Joumana being one of them. Mike Fleming mentally 'phewed' a sigh of relief as the enlarged group, dispensing with formalities, commenced an evening of hilarious joke recitals accompanied by illustrative acting. It culminated in promises to meet up again next Friday.

A shrill shriek pierced the relative calm of Rue Yamount as Sami slammed the casement window firmly shut. A slumbering tomcat, sunning itself on the projecting window sill, was a fraction too late escaping and the tip of its tail jammed between the mating surfaces of the window frame. Omar had completed the remaining investigations and had delivered the results the previous night. Sami had had a pressing engagement and had delayed checking the results against the projects list provided by Solidere. Building 121 appeared in the projects list and the details complied with the fragmented information contained in the torn exercise book. The closing date for Submission of Tenders had been 10.30 a.m. that morning. Sami knew he was too late. The formal Opening of Tenders was conducted behind closed doors to permit certain flexibilities in placing the contract award, prior to the public announcements, made the following day. Solidere had adopted a rigid policy of transparency in all of their commercial dealings but they had found deep-rooted traditions hard to eradicate. Sami pondered the problem as the tomcat, tail wedged between frame and casement, screamed in agony.

Samantha's holiday was rapidly coming to an end. She was having a wonderful time, skiing most days and savouring the nightlife of Beirut most nights. Felicity had initially loaned her daughter the 4 x 4 so that she had independence of movement. It had been her second day on the piste, arrayed in her multicoloured ski suit, when she had met George. The chairlifts to the higher slopes are designed for three people. Jostling for position at the turnstile, she found herself sharing the chair with a tall, handsome young man, the third space remaining vacant. As is the custom in Lebanon, the young man immediately fell into conversation. George was typical of many Lebanese young men from wealthy families. He had received his further education in America and on graduating with a Master's Degree in Business Administration had returned to Lebanon to help run the family business. He drove a Mercedes coupé, was lithe and graceful, possessed a wicked sense of humour, and radiated energy. Samantha, initially abashed at his informality soon realised that it was a cultural thing; nobody stood on ceremony here; everybody seemed to know everybody else. The atmosphere at the ski lodge and in the milling crowd of skiers jostling for position at the chair lift turnstiles was instant party atmosphere. Laughter was everywhere. Samantha felt comfortable with these people, and without realising it soon became one of them. George was a gentleman. He asked nothing more than Samantha's companionship, and for the remainder of the holiday Samantha and George expended enormous amounts of energy in the day on the slopes, and even more during the nights, wining, dining and dancing until the early hours, each night at a more colourful venue.

Their last night together had been spectacular. They had rendezvoused at Samantha's parents' apartment at 9 p.m. Both Felicity and John had taken an immediate liking to George (there really was nothing to dislike) and they had no qualms about the casual relationship. George gunned the Mercedes as it ascended the tortuous winding mountain road, the vehicle growling and snarling as it warned the bevy of ancient asthmatic vehicles to 'make way' for this king of cars. The mountain road levelled off at Wakim's Supermarket and they motored across the mountain plateau through dense pine forests. Soon they commenced a brief descent. Across the valley, Samantha saw clusters of twinkling lights signifying tiny mountain villages. The air smelt of pine and the tranquillity was so powerful that she snuggled closer into the padded passenger seat. Sweeping around a sharp bend, the vehicle's headlights illuminated a gigantic property surrounded by well-tended pine trees. Samantha caught her breath as she regarded the Arabian Castle with awe. Dark profiles of multi-sized onion-shaped roofs appeared, capped in black with curved turrets. Lights shone from oriel windows as they peeked into the night through multi-paned eyes. The majesty of the building was awe-inspiring. George abruptly halted the Mercedes at the foot of a magnificent floodlit staircase that meandered upwards towards an enormous Arabic headed entrance.

'George,' breathed Samantha, 'what is this place?'

George laughed. 'This, my dear sweet Sam, is "Janna". It is where we shall spend the remainder of your holiday.'

Tossing the car keys to a waiting parking attendant, George took Samantha's hand and they ascended passing into the bowels of 'Janna' through the massive, cedar-wood twin front doors, where until the early hours enjoyed the many promised delights of an Oriental Experience…

That night Samantha realised the meaning of 'Eastern promise', and she responded to the experiences with gusto. She hoped the evening would never end. The night sky was lightening as the tired but happy couple descended the magnificent staircase to the waiting car. The journey back was uneventful. Farewells were made and as Samantha watched the taillights of George's Mercedes recede, she smiled aware that the holiday romance was now over.

'I will never forget you, George,' she said to herself. With a final glance at the now deserted road, she made her way up to her parents' apartment. Her flight was scheduled to depart that morning at 7.30 a.m. Packing took no time. Her emotional farewell with her parents took longer. At five o'clock, the hooting of a horn disturbed the family gathering. The taxi had arrived. John had offered to drive her but Samantha hated goodbyes and had refused. She found the pain of parting unbearable. As the Middle East Airways airbus thrust itself noisily up and away from Beirut International Airport into a perfect blue sky, Samantha, lodged in her window seat, looked down on tiny Lebanon with its snow capped mountains, shimmering in the early morning sunshine, with heart-tugging desire. Tears welling up, she quietly said to herself 'Au revoir, my *Habibtih*; thanks for such a wonderful time.'

Arriving back at Heathrow Airport, she found Giles waiting. Samantha looked absolutely radiant, he thought, as they embraced.

★

Omar was in a quandary. Sami had not contacted him for a couple of days and with the investigation complete, he was unsure what to do with the model of Beirut Central District that took up most of the only bedroom in his family apartment. The alternative accommodation arrangements for his family had proved satisfactory. They had settled in well, were well entrenched, and showed little inclination to return. As a consequence, Omar's diet had suffered. Previously tight-fitting trousers were now hanging loose from a diminishing waistline.

Later that week, the *Daily Star* reported a seemingly unrelated event, included in a small paragraph tucked away at the bottom of page six. There had been another break-in in the Foch-Allenby area. Little damage had been caused, as only the front door lock had been forced. A stolen model of the Beirut Central District had been returned. The police were mystified. It caused no reaction from the general public; the police placed the file in 'Case Solved Records', and Omar's family returned home.

Sami had obtained the name of the successful contractor awarded the Solidere package which included Building 121. He had already met with Lili Ghaddar, the owner of Beirut Construction Company (BCC), and had offered to execute the whole of the works relating to Building 121 on a sub-contract basis. Lili, Salem Ghaddar's widow, had inherited the company on the death of her husband, was intent on driving a hard bargain. She didn't like Sami, but the additional money would be useful. She had young Joseph (her Armenian toyboy) to keep happy. His demands were forever escalating. Preliminary overtures had already commenced, and Sami was resigned to the final haggling extending over the next couple of weeks. Sami mused, What did it matter – so long as he had first access to the building. Anyway Sami knew about the arrangement between Lili and Joseph, and although she intended to extract a princely sum from him, he felt confident that he could use the relationship to his benefit. What worried him more was that Solidere's approval to the arrangements was necessary. Sami knew he would have to dig deep into his pockets.

John, armed with his own and the two Mike's measurements, had been on a shopping spree in Central Hamra. He purchased three pairs of multi-pocketed trousers, three shooting jackets and a small rucksack. These were stored in the apartment next to the articles purchased in London.

Chapter 9

Ian and Simon enjoyed a relatively uneventful flight to Heathrow, other than slight air turbulence over Turkey and an over attentive cabin steward. Simon had occupied the aisle seat in Business Class, and as the flight progressed, the middle-aged cabin steward kept popping up out of nowhere to enquire in a preposterously precious voice, marred with a slight lisp, if Simon had everything he needed. The question seemed to end in a moist, unspoken question mark. Much to Simon's embarrassment, terms of casual endearment crept into the 'enquiries' over France. The MEA flight landed at Heathrow Airport on time and taxied to its parking bay.

Ian had slept for most of the journey. The attentive steward's forceful fumbling with Ian's seat belt had jolted him into consciousness. Passing from the aircraft's exit door into the passenger embarkation tunnel, Simon was forced to run the gauntlet of the bunched cabin crew. He reddened as the steward, bidding farewell, silently blew him a kiss. Ian and Simon marched into the terminal, passed through passport control, entered baggage reclamation and having collected their suitcases, exited customs without any bother and entered the public arrivals section. There, waiting at the barrier, Ian spied Janette. With a brief handshake, Simon left Ian to make his own way back to London.

Ian embraced Janette. There then followed an unusual silence. It had been Ian's first trip abroad, and the strange environment of the bustling airport placed unaccustomed restraints on the intimacy of the married couple. Janette eventually broke the silence. 'Ian... oh, you look terribly well! Did you have a good trip?'

Ian, dapper in his dark business suit, a slight suntan on his generally pallid face, replied, 'Yes, dear, it was most interesting... How are the children?'

Casual passers-by would have seen a slightly overweight woman, clutching an enormous handbag in the company of a medium-height, tubby businessman, with pigskin brief case in one hand, worry beads in the other, and wearing a red fez with the tassel hanging over one eye. The religious inclinations of the man may have caused a few subconsciously raised eyebrows.

Ian and Janette broke their journey home by lunching at the Barley Mow public house, located in a quiet street off Dorking Market Square. A serious argument had been avoided by Ian's concession not to wear his fez in the pub, but nothing Janette could say would part him from his worry beads. Lunch was consumed in companionable silence. Arriving back at Chartway, Ian felt the slight pang of remorse as he confronted the family home and the associated rigid routine of family and business life. It had been such fun, he thought to himself as he contemplated the prospects of tomorrow. He couldn't confide in Janette the revulsion he was beginning to feel for the routine. 'Ugh!' he said to himself.

'What did you say Ian?' Janette asked.

'Oh – nothing dear,' he replied.

Greeting Ian as he parked the car in the drive were Alexander and William. Bowling him over in their rush to be first, the two children badgered him incessantly by asking questions like, 'Where've you been?' 'Got any presents for us?'

As Ian handed over the gifts, Alexander shouted, 'William, that's mine!'

'Stop it, it's not fair,' whined William and the squabbling started about the size of their respective presents.

Janette's mum had been babysitting, and she had made afternoon tea, so at three o'clock in the afternoon, with the English weather closing in, Ian sat in his lounge drinking endless cups of English breakfast tea, watching the drizzle running down the windowpanes, whilst Janette's mother chattered ceaselessly about important local events. Neither Ian nor Janette listened to the catalogue of complaints about the weather, supermarket prices, the antics of Mrs Brown at the Housewives Register meeting and Mrs Roe-Bottom's scene in Smith's. The children played happily, albeit noisily, in the playroom with their computer games. Ian was still 2,500 miles away whilst Janette was contemplating the most recent happening. She was becoming seriously disturbed. The most recent of these strange events had occurred on the second day of Ian's absence abroad. She had been doing the weekly wash when the front doorbell jingled. Opening the door, she was confronted with an official-looking little man clutching a clipboard.

'Good morning,' the little man said. 'Am I talking to Mrs McEwan?' he enquired.

'Well, yes,' Janette said.

'Good morning Madam, my name is Arthur Portly. I'm from the local Social Services Office. May I come in?' The fluency of this speech was impeded by a slight stutter.

'What is this about?' asked Janette.

'I would prefer to discuss the matter, which is rather delicate, in the privacy of your home, rather than on the doorstep, if you don't mind.' The words exploded with little 'pops' as Arthur Portly struggled to get them out.

'Oh well, if you must,' replied Janette, and she ushered the little man into the confines of the hall, leaving the front door ajar, just in case there was any funny business.

'Is your husband at home?' continued Arthur Portly once they were beyond the vision of prying eyes.

'No, he's abroad at the moment,' replied Janette. 'Why do you ask?'

'I have to get all the facts,' retorted the little man, struggling with the word 'facts'.

'What facts? What are you talking about?' demanded Janette.

'Well,' the little man continued, 'this is rather delicate, but we have received reports that your husband may be, how can I put this, not respecting his obligations to his family...' The effort of stringing this sentence together had made Mr Arthur Portly go red in the face, but he persisted. 'According to our reports, your husband has been acting very strangely. Under Government legislation we are required to investigate all possible cases of child abuse. You will appreciate we take the opportunity to nip these situations in the bud and offer counselling. It is only as a last resort that we take children to foster homes.' Arthur Portly's face had turned purple.

Janette was flabbergasted. What's this silly little man talking about? she thought to herself. Converting her thoughts into a verbal tirade she towered over Arthur Portly, bosoms thrust out, as she assaulted him with an avalanche of, *'What?' 'Why?'* and *'What on earth are you talking about?'* Arthur Portly physically shrank back into a corner.

'Please, Mrs McEwan, you must understand we are here to help you. We can investigate wife abuse, so if your husband is mistreating you, please, we know people who can help.' His stutter had become more apparent as he gasped to get the words out.

Janette lost control of herself. Grabbing the clipboard from his hand, she proceeded to hit Arthur Portly over the head. 'You stupid man!' she cried. 'What are you saying? Get out of my house. *Get out, get out!'*

With that, Mr Arthur Portly was unceremoniously shoved out of the front door, his clipboard following. 'Mrs McEwan,' he stuttered, standing bedraggled on the front porch. 'We also investigate cases of husband abuse!' he screamed, as the front door slammed in his face.

The neighbours' curtains twitched at this news. Coffee morning chatter would be enlivened for the next couple of weeks as unseeing eyes watched the Social Services Officer, retrieve his clip board from the flower bed where it had landed and slowly limped his way towards the bus stop at the end of the road. As he walked, he scribbled nervously at the Social Security Form Number 9211701, clipped to his clipboard, writing around the spots of clinging earth.

Janette was beside herself. 'What was he talking about?' she asked herself for the rest of the morning. That afternoon at Mrs. Sherbet's 'coffee morning', she was greeted with cool reserve from her friends and found herself excluded from the general hum of conversation, which was conducted today in low tones, with accompanying glances in her general direction. Janette suddenly felt terribly lonely. That evening, after the children had gone to bed and Mum had left, Janette recounted the episode of

Mr Arthur Portly to Ian. Neither of them could understand what was happening.

The following morning Ian, dressed in his traditional business suit, garnished now with gaudy socks, flamboyant tie, fez and worry beads, boarded the 7.15 to Charing Cross. His entry into his normal compartment was greeted by a stunned silence. His travelling companions exchanged surreptitious looks before burying themselves in their copies of *The Times*. Further rumours were conceived during the journey to London Bridge, all unknown to Ian. On reaching the office Ian made a telephone call to his local Social Security Office. Mr Arthur Portly had made a formal complaint about the assault. Ian was requested to visit the office the next morning to discuss the matter with Mr Dick Foreskin, Mr Portly's supervisor. The office routine soon engulfed Ian, and his memories faded as the pressure of work forced them away.

*

Setting up the site investigation had been more difficult than John had anticipated. He had spoken with Wajid Chehayed, Solidere's Project Manager, requesting authorisation to visit the site of Building 121 on the following day. Wajid, dispensing his inevitable joke as a prelude to serious talk, couldn't understand John's request for three passes. 'Why three passes, John?' he queried. 'You know that the site investigation should have been concluded seven weeks ago. What's happened to warrant a visit at this late stage?' Wajid, notwithstanding his childish sense of humour, was highly intelligent.

John had already concocted his story, and it was with consummate ease that he leant back in his chair and lied convincingly, eyes wandering towards Rola as he did so.

Finally Wajid relented, 'I shouldn't be doing this, you know. We have had very strict instructions from up high. The company has suffered greatly from theft. Nobody is allowed on site, other than Solidere's personnel and Ministry Officials. If a contractor is there, his workforce are all screened every time they pass the security gate. The whole area is littered with buried Roman antiquities, not to mention some of the architectural gems in the buildings. In the right hands these could bring culture and wealth to Lebanon. But that's not the point. These antiquities are Lebanon's heritage, which is being plundered, and my bosses want it stopped. But okay, I'll authorise you and your other specialists entry permits for tomorrow. Please let me know the results of the investigation. I do find it quite extraordinary that you suspect that the building has a major structural fault. The structural survey showed nothing. I suppose it is possible that after the last small earthquake the building is now leaning. Perhaps we could open it to the tourists. I can see the placards: "Visit the Leaning Tower: The new SLANT to Beirut".' With that, chuckling away to himself, he replaced the receiver.

John gave a sigh of relief. He had planned the visit to coincide with bad weather. John strode to the window and glanced out. Black storm clouds were billowing in from the sea, the wind was rising and the temperature was dropping. As John left the office for his homeward trek, he felt the first few drops of rain. By the time he reached Mansourieh, gale force conditions had enveloped the country.

Sami regarded the aging woman with an expression of frustration. The bloody woman can't make up her mind, he thought to himself. He had responded aggressively to the opening of the negotiations, and over the days the differences had been narrowed. He had lost count of the number of cups of coffee he had consumed. As soon as Sami thought he had a deal, Lili would produce another condition and the whole ritual would start all over again. Already he had conceded far more than he could afford. Doubt began to assail him as to whether it was worth the gamble. Sitting here with this bloody woman day after day, drinking coffee and making small talk, waiting for the first opening gambit of the negotiations, then having to thrust in and out with proposals and counter-proposals wasn't his kind of fun. The trouble is, he thought to himself, I can't anticipate her next move. She's bouncing around like a ping-pong ball…

Lili's mind was wandering. Joseph was being a bore. He had established himself in her sumptuous apartment about six months ago. The initial novelty of living with an older woman had soon worn off and it was only the treats that brought him to heel; and these were now getting out of proportion, she thought to herself. His more recent demand had been a nearly new Porsche. She had refused and had suffered his rejection for a couple of nights. Thinking that she could squeeze the additional money out of Sami she had negotiated hard only to find that Joseph had subsequently changed his mind. He now wanted nothing from her at all. Demands rocked between the ridiculous and the sublime.

The following morning fully met John's expectations. A belt of low pressure was affecting the Eastern Mediterranean, and Lebanon was shrouded in low cloud with intermittent heavy rain showers. It was a cold, blustery sort of day with generally poor visibility. John arrived at the Café Mondo, the pre- arranged meeting point, a little before 8 a.m. The restaurant was busy with dedicated early morning joggers, who having completed their daily exercise programmes on the Corniche, had come in to enjoy the delights of the first meal of the day in the companionship of friends and in the warmth of the restaurant. Sweaty clothes, discarded over empty chairs, exuded offensive smells, testifying to the rigid daily ritual. But as one entered the restaurant, the rich aroma of fresh coffee assailed the olfactory senses, masking the other odours within the immediate vicinity.

The Café Mondo was located on the ground floor and at one end of the newly refurbished Phoenicia Hotel. Selecting a table with views of the main hotel entrance, John watched the convoy of extremely expensive chauffeur-driven motorcars as they swished in and out of the curved entrance pick-up point, collecting dignitaries, businessmen or tourists with the frequency of a clock's ticking second hand. The ringing of advancing footsteps on the stone tiles announced the arrival of Mike Brady. A few minutes later Mike Fleming joined them.

'Sorry I'm late, you guys! Had a bit of a do last night,' Mike said, as he eyed the young waitress who had presented herself at the table to take their orders. With a mind switching from past excuses to present opportunities, Mike Fleming immediately engaged the young lady in conversation as to the variety of coffees available on the menu. Settling with espressos all round, Mike watched the shapely legs retreat as the young waitress waltzed her way to the kitchen.

'Why don't you give it a rest?' Mike Brady growled. 'At this hour in the morning, your antics border on the obscene.'

'Oh you know how it is, Mike, or perhaps you don't. I just can't resist a pretty face,' retorted Mike.

Both John and Mike grinned and in unison said, 'Yes Mike, we know!'

The arrival of steaming coffee broke the flow of conversation while each man sipped the hot drink. As they drained the dregs of their respective cups, John said, 'Okay, guys, lets do it. Mike, as you fancy the waitress, perhaps you'll pay the bill and we'll meet up at Mike Brady's 4 x 4, which is parked over there.' He pointed in a general direction. 'Please double-check you've brought everything. We can't have a repeat performance.'

Rendezvousing at Mike's vehicle some ten minutes later, the equipment was checked and stored in the back of the vehicle. Slamming the tailgate shut, Mike got into the driver's seat, started the engine and slipped the transmission into drive. They soon entered the early morning traffic flow to downtown Beirut. They were held up at some traffic lights for a couple of minutes due to a logjam of vehicles.

'What's wrong with these people?' John shouted. 'For God's sake, it's all so bloody simple. If the lights are red, you stop. If they are green, you go. How can you have a traffic logjam at traffic lights?'

Apparently, a few years previously, the Lebanese Government had employed a traffic consultant to sort out traffic congestion and identify rules. He was a French national who had personally been quite successful in reducing the incidence of traffic road rage in a number of European capitals. His recommendations to the Government had been brief. 'He could do nothing,' said the Report. 'The Lebanese drivers have no respect for authority and they do exactly as they wish.'

The congestion at the crossroads eventually cleared on the arrival of a policeman on a motorcycle. Mike parked his vehicle outside the compound, and Mike, Mike and John unloaded the survey equipment. Protected against the weather (it was now raining again), they made their way towards the security gate, each man shouldering some of the equipment. This comprised a dumpy level with tripod and three of four stout-looking ranging rods. Cameras and notebooks were packed into the small rucksack casually slung over John's shoulder.

The three men chatted amicably with the group of young soldiers during the brief security check. There was little to examine. Each man was wearing heavy protective clothing, and besides the small rucksack there was no place for concealment. The officer in charge laughed at one of John's jokes as they were ushered into the inner compound, little interest being taken in the equipment. The ruined city, a cemetery of past glories embalmed in its own misery, took no notice as the three men threaded their way through the rubble-strewn streets in their passage to Building 121. Building 121 looked little different from adjacent buildings. The five-storey block, embellished with cracked and crazed limestone carvings, displayed its wounds with a sorrowful air. Adding to the general atmosphere of gloom was the torrential rain now falling. It had once been a proud edifice erected during the last century by skilled craftsmen. Some of its past magnificence was still vaguely discernable under the layers of grime. Whilst it had suffered war-damage, it was the general air of neglect and deterioration that contributed to the oppressive atmosphere of gloom and despondency. Solidere had already established that structurally the building was relatively sound. Extensive renovations were necessary to transform the derelict ruin into a modern building, cloaked in its original façade. The survey necessitated measuring the vertical alignment of the structure, accompanied by a detailed inspection of the fabric to identify whether cracking was of such significance that it would affect the building's structural stability. The survey would be performed generally outside. Around the site, at regular intervals, Solidere had installed CCTV cameras, and the three men were fully aware that their every movement was being watched and recorded. After setting up the equipment, they all went into their respective song and dance routines, mainly for the benefit of the watching cameras. The day gradually brightened and around 1 p.m. they decided that it would be a good idea to break for lunch. Arriving back at the security gate, the personal search was a little more thorough, but nothing was found and they were allowed to exit. Each man was carrying a ranging rod. Arriving at the parked vehicle, these were thrown into the back. Within a few seconds, the guard detail watched as the vehicle pulled away from the kerb into the main traffic stream and accelerated towards Beirut City. The lunchtime arrangements had been pre-planned down to the smallest detail. Arriving at a small lock-up garage, Mike drove the vehicle into the enclosed space, pulling the 'up and over' garage door down behind them.

Two hours later, the three men again presented themselves at the security gate. They went though the same procedure as previously, prior to being ushered into the main compound. The rain had stopped and the clouds were lifting. It promised to be a pleasant afternoon. Arriving back at Building 121, they continued the survey, completing the survey around 5 p.m. The survey equipment looked heavy as the security men watched the three men approach the gate. The men looked tired, and arriving at the Security Office, they failed to respond to the soldiers' overtures. Offers of Arabic coffee were refused and they looked nervous as they were checked out. Finding nothing, the Security Officer waved them through. He watched the backs of the retreating men as they walked towards the parked vehicle, opened the tail-gate and deposited the equipment in the back. He made notes in his daily log, closed the book and resumed watching the local football match being televised by LBC.

The three men unloaded the vehicle in the secure confines of the rented garage. By 7 p.m. the operation was concluded. Bidding each other farewell, they departed to their respective destinations; Mike Fleming to a date with a lovely young creature; Mike Brady to the loneliness of his apartment, (another evening watching TV); and John to his beloved wife, Felicity. They had agreed that the following night they would all meet up at the

Mayflower Hotel. It wasn't Friday, so they could be assured of a quiet evening drinking.

Sami sensed that Lili's concentration was even more erratic today than yesterday. Joseph had moved out of Lili's apartment the previous night. They had had a row. Joseph had resumed making outrageous demands, insisting that he should be allowed to bring his younger sister to live with them. 'Family relationships were so important don't you think?' he concluded.

Lili, goaded into fury by his insensitivity towards her, finally rounded on Joseph. 'What sister? You have no sister! What is she, one of your occasional whores that you wish to contaminate my home with? Do you think I'm a stupid old cow? No, I will not have her in my house, nor will I have you. Get out. Go on, get out!' she screamed. 'You no longer please me.'

For the remainder of the evening, Joseph had cooed to her behind Lili's closed bedroom door. He poured out heart-rending endearments in a voice rich with velvet charm. He expounded his adorations for her, his love for her alone, that she was God's chosen mate for him. He concluded at midnight that he could never consider being unfaithful to her; that she was the sun of his life; and so it went on, deep into the night, the gentle voice pleading for forgiveness.

The negotiations with Sami were taking their toll on Lili. In a more balanced frame of mind, Joseph and Lili would have been reconciled that evening. Sami's inherent brutality distorted the fine balance between the right and wrong decisions and later, Lili would regret what she had done. Through the closed bedroom door, Lili had firmly told Joseph to leave; she never wanted to see him again.

Sami struck his bargain at midday with a distraught Lili. Sami couldn't quite comprehend why she now accepted a deal that was inferior to one he had made a couple of days previously. The workings of a woman's mind was of little consequence to Sami. He had his building. The loss would be less than he had anticipated. To circumvent any problems, they had agreed that Sami would provide seconded labour and management experience to Lili's company on the package containing Building 121. Works were scheduled to start in three days' time. Back in his own office, Sami rubbed his hands in glee. He had access to Building 121; he had been formally invited to tender for the second building on the list and he had identified the other two buildings. They would be subject to tender within the next six months. For the first time in months Sami radiated a resemblance of bonhomie. Picking up the telephone, he called Omar, acknowledging the fact that Omar had not been paid in months.

'Just get over here before 10 a.m.,' he said, 'if you want to get paid.' Ignoring Omar's pleadings that he had a part-time job down at the fish market, he put the telephone down.

Chapter 10

Once formal permission had been granted to the appointed contractor to visit the site, Lili had agreed that Sami would proceed to conduct the initial site investigation to determine the extent and scope of temporary works necessary to renovate the old building. Sami had insisted on this condition and his mind was currently mulling over the problems of secreting the gold bullion (if found) away from the site under the noses of the security guards. He had bounced various ideas off Omar, but so far the only system that had appealed had been generated by his memories of the James Bond film, *Gold Finger*. Omar had suggested casting the bullion into concrete test cubes. It was permissible to conduct concrete testing by independent testing laboratories 'off site'. Sami had rejected the idea, as he wanted immediate recovery of the gold. He had measured the diameter of the petrol intake on his old Mercedes. It was adequate to receive gold sovereigns, and once they'd been deposited in the petrol tank, the vehicle could be transported to a selected garage, the tank stripped and the bullion retrieved. The only problem was the visibility of this activity to the site CCTV cameras. He needed concealment from prying eyes.

Saturday merged into Sunday and still Sami had not bettered the idea of concealing the bullion. Sunday night was spent closeted with Omar as they made final plans. They had agreed that Sami and Omar would gain access to the site, using Sami's old Mercedes; the others would follow later. As the Lebanese never walk anywhere, the security guards would not be suspicious. Passage to the building would be difficult due to the rubble strewn over the ground, but Sami had already discounted this problem, Omar could always clear the way.

Monday dawned bright and beautiful. As Sami's wall-mounted cuckoo clock cuckooed the hour, culminating at 'eight' with strangled base gurgling noises, Sami drowned the dregs of his Arabic coffee, replaced the tiny cup on its equally diminutive saucer, his eyes straying to the chaotic pile of torn exercise pages festooned about his desk. Each was covered with Arabic scribble, crossings out, ink blotches and grubby fingerprints. His plan was made. He was excited as he levered himself out of his study chair. As if to gain momentum to his upward thrust, a conveniently timed burst of flatus blasted its way through his tightly bunched, bulbous buttock cheeks, billowed his loose fitting trousers to an obscene shape, until it finally escaped through his trouser legs as he moved with mincing steps towards the study door.

Exiting his house, he walked towards the ancient Mercedes, parked haphazardly on the pavement. The car started immediately, and with the initial surge of power he engaged 'drive' and swung out into the passing traffic, oblivious to the screeching of brakes behind and the angry 'raspberry' sound of horns protesting at his unannounced entry into the early morning traffic. Sami had had the same old Mercedes for many years. He could not relate to the younger generation who chose their cars with care as symbols of their station; their women were selected to match the colour scheme of the chosen vehicle. Sami drove carelessly, threading his way through the rapidly moving traffic, lane discipline forgotten as something peculiar to other countries. Arriving at the BCD district, he parked immediately adjacent to the main security gate to await the arrival of Omar.

Omar's belated arrival was announced by a cloud of flies and the 'putt-putt' sound of his Vespa scooter (borrowed from his cousin). Omar had worked the early morning shift down at the fish market; there had been inadequate time to shower and change. Leaning the scooter against a handy lamppost, Omar approached Sami's parked vehicle, followed religiously by a cloud of buzzing flies. Grasping the passenger door handle, Omar yanked the door open and, as he prepared to slide into the passenger seat, Sami lent across, grabbed the armrest and slammed the door shut, shouting as he did so, 'Omar, you stink to high heaven! You had better walk.'

The last part of the sentence was muffled behind the slammed door. With resignation, Omar turned and made his way towards the security gate followed by the spluttering of the old vehicle as it edged its way towards the closed gate.

Entering a side gate, Omar confronted the security guard. Proximity of body contact was kept at the maximum distance possible for the guard to take the proffered papers from Omar's out-stretched hand. 'Wa-ef hone! – Stop here!' the guard commanded to Omar, as he returned to his office to receive instructions. Sami watched through the starred windscreen as the guard made his telephone call to Solidere's Main Office. Replacing the telephone, the guard viewed Omar with suspicion, but operated the electric mechanism and the main gate slowly swung back on its hinges. Sami gave a silent sigh of relief. He nudged the Mercedes between the gateposts until, well inside the security zone, he turned off the engine, got out of the car and went to get directions as to the whereabouts of Building 121. The guard, pleased at the prospect of an early morning chat, extended normal greetings and soon he and Sami were deep in conversation. Omar kept a discreet distance. Eventually Sami was satisfied that he could locate Building 121 and, passing the information on to Omar, restarted the car.

Progress was uneventful, other than the constant pauses whilst Omar manually cleared the numerous obstacles out of the way, to allow passage. Finally, Sami saw Building 121, identified by a white painted number high up on the external face of the wall. Stopping the car immediately outside the derelict building, Sami got out and walked into the gloomy interior. Could this be it? he wondered to himself. His excitement had mounted and he was now passing wind at a prodigious rate. He looked around his surroundings. All the windows had been boarded up and what little light there was entered by way of shell holes in the external wall. They provided shafts of sunshine, spotlighting selected areas. The interior was as silent as a grave, and exuded the feeling of a vast, long-dead cadaver in whose bowels Sami now stood. He remembered old Amin Hakim's description of the location of the bullion box: '…1 metre down… under… carved…'

It was clear that the box must be concealed on the ground floor and that it was near some sort of carving. He felt flies settling on his face. Looking up, he saw Omar standing near by.

'Go and keep lookout, Omar,' Sami said. 'Act as if you are inspecting the façade.'

With Omar's departure, the irritating flies disappeared and Sami was able to concentrate. He cursed himself for forgetting to bring a torch but he had his pocket lighter. The illumination provided by this was feeble, but he was able to shuffle from room to room in his search for a carving. The interior of the building was a mess. Debris and rubble littered the ground floor. The internal walls generally stood, many with gaping holes following the trajectory of shells passing through them. Internal doors and their frames had disappeared, no doubt scavenged by the homeless to feed their winter fires. The floor above was generally intact but the once elaborate carved staircase had been amputated at the first landing and the upper part hung crazily down from the first floor stairwell void.

Where would they install something 'carved'?' Sami mused, as he wandered around the decrepit building. Filth was everywhere, and as Sami brushed against concealed obstructions, an observer would have noticed that his profile was gradually vanishing as he blended into the dirty grey gloom. His eyes ranged across the walls, his tiny lighter throwing out a flickering light. Suddenly he caught sight of a carved stone lintel over one of the empty doorways. Rushing towards it, he stumbled on the corner of some projecting object. Stooping, heart beating rapidly, he rummaged around the filthy debris. His hand touched something solid and immoveable. Mounting excitement shot through his body as he struggled to remove the object but it was firmly embedded in the floor. Quickly he called to Omar to bring a shovel or other implement. He had to repeat the instruction three times, each in ascending decibels before the presence of flies indicated that Omar had arrived. Unable to adjust his vision rapidly to the interior gloom, Omar thrust a hard object into Sami's face.

'You fool!' Sami snarled. 'Give it to me.' Sami took hold of a round hard object. He discovered that Omar had brought a broom. Forcing the handle into a gap between the object and the surrounding floor, Sami leant his weight onto the projecting end. He was rewarded with a sharp crack as the wooden handle broke.

'Get something else, you idiot!' Sami roared. 'Get a tyre lever from the boot of the car!'

Omar disappeared, evidenced by the rapid decrease in flies. Sami again tried to insert the shorter length of the boom shaft into the gap and lever the object out into the open. This time he applied more gentle pressure and the object moved. Wriggling the handle around the side of the object, Sami detected that movement was becoming more pronounced and by the time Omar had returned, Sami had levered a box out of its nesting place.

'Omar!' barked Sami, 'lift the box and take it over there.'

Sami had pointed in the general direction of one of the rays of sunshine. Unable to see where Sami was pointing, Omar bent forward, lifted the box, straightened, turned and walked straight into an adjacent wall.

'Fool!' snarled Sami. 'Here, let me have it.'

Passing a solid object from one pair of hands to another is a relatively simple exercise. The box missed Sami's outstretched hands and it hit the floor with a crash. Omar squealed in pain, hopping around on one leg as he grasped the other, holding his bruised toes. The floor did not afford a solid footing, and during one of Omar's hops, his good foot rolled on a lump of rubble and with a crash, he knocked into Sami, bounced, ricocheted off the wall and finally ended spreadeagled in the rubble, covered with filth from the floor.

On impact with Omar, Sami's lighter had spiralled out of his grasp and they were both plunged into darkness. Omar cautiously sat up.

'Get up, you fool!' Sami snarled. 'Take the box over to that spot of light.'

Heaving and grunting, Omar carried it into the shaft of sunshine. They clearly saw that the object was indeed an ammunition box. Sami's heart leapt. *I've got it*, he thought. *It must contain my missing bullion.*

'Open it,' he barked.

'I can't,' bleated Omar.

'Why not?' retorted Sami.

'You can see it's padlocked,' replied Omar. Sami cursed out loud. Of course it would be padlocked, all shipments were padlocked, he thought. 'Use the tyre lever you fool!' he told Omar.

Returning to the spot where they had found the box, Omar groped around in the debris until finally he found the metal bar. Retracing his way back to Sami, he bent down and inserted the lever between the hasp and staple and was just about to apply pressure when they heard voices outside. Sami's fury erupted. The other members of the inspection team had arrived early.

'Omar – quick, hide the box in that dark corner. Cover it with debris and sit on it. If somebody comes in and sees you, say, you don't feel very well. I'll go outside and see them,' Sami said over his shoulder, on his way out to remonstrate with the new arrivals. The sound of raised voices echoed throughout the building.

After some time, the sound of voices diminished and Omar heard footsteps approaching his hiding place.

'Omar where are you?' he heard Sami whisper.

'Over here,' replied Omar in a quiet voice.

'Where's "over here", you fool? I can't see you,' Sami replied.

'Oh well, it doesn't matter. I've told them to confine their inspection to the outside. We have about thirty minutes before they come into the building.'

'But you said we would be alone,' whispered Omar.

'I know what I said,' Sami replied. Apparently Lili had forgotten to tell her own inspection team and they had arrived with the Solidere Project Manager.

'What do we do now?' said Omar.

'*Think*,' answered Sami. His mind was whirling. His carefully made plans were falling apart. He had this one opportunity to retrieve the bullion. Once the other men entered the building all would be lost. He had to make the most of this precious half-hour.

'What size is the box?' asked Sami.

'It's quite large,' replied Omar.

'I know it's quite large, but what size is it?' questioned Sami.

'I don't know,' repeated Omar.

'Are you wearing a belt?' asked Sami.

'Well yes, my trousers would fall down otherwise!'

'Yes I know that. Take off your coat and undo your belt,' instructed Sami.

'But my trousers will fall down,' protested Omar.

'Just do as I say!' snarled Sami.

Omar stood in the dark corner, trousers crumpled around his ankles, waiting for the next instruction.

'Come over here and bring the box,' commanded Sami.

Shuffling across the floor, Omar dragged himself and the box into the light. Sami had calculated that if they could lift the box onto Omar's back it could be secured in place by the belt and concealed from prying eyes by the coat. It would give Omar the appearance of a hunchback, but what was the alternative? They had to take the risk. He would pretend that Omar had been taken sick and required immediate medical treatment. With Omar's back bent double, they hoisted the box onto his back until it was evenly balanced. Then Sami secured it in place with the belt and threw Omar's coat over it.

Omar groaned. 'I can't do this,' he protested.

Sami ignored him. 'I'll support you. Lean on me.'

Together they slowly weaved their way through the building like a pantomime horse, Omar resting his chest on Sami' s bent buttocks. The box kept on slipping and they had to stop to make adjustments every now and then.

'Stop here,' Sami whispered, as they neared the entrance. Leaving Omar to cope with the excessive load as best he could, Sami straightened up and took a quick look outside. The other men's voices were quite audible, but as luck had it, they were on the blind side of the building.

'Okay, it's clear. Come on,' Sami whispered.

The site CCTV cameras would show, later that day, the extraordinary spectacle of two men, both crouched double, tottering across the open space between building and car, followed by a cloud of flies. Fortunately, as they approached the old Mercedes, it gave cover from the CCTV cameras. Grasping the rear passenger door handle, Sami yanked the door open, and turning, pushed Omar into the open space. Grabbing flailing legs, he forced them into the vehicle and slammed the door. His timing was impeccable, as at that moment, the other men rounded the corner of the building and came into sight.

'What's the matter?' came a general enquiry.

'Omar's sick or something.' Sami replied, 'I've got to take him to hospital immediately.'

'Is it serious? Can we help?' one of the men asked.

'No, it's best left to the doctor. I should go now, for Omar's sake,' replied Sami. His appearance had deteriorated since his early morning arrival at Building 121. His smart suit was crumpled and filthy. It was covered in moving black spots. Every now and then a couple of black specks would launch themselves into the air, buzz around his dishevelled hair a couple of times, to alight in a new place – only to repeat the process a couple of seconds later.

The men stared at the strange figure but their attention was soon distracted by the antics of the Mercedes. It was moving up and down in an unsynchronised rolling motion, accompanied by muffled screams. As one of the men later remarked, it sounded like a pop singer encased in a tin can. Not waiting for any response, Sami opened the car door, slid into the driver's seat, started the vehicle and disappeared into the distance, leaving the men aghast.

The privacy within the vehicle gave Sami the opportunity to think through his next step. He had to run the gauntlet of passing through the security gate. He reasoned that if he pleaded that Omar had fallen and was badly hurt, they could avoid the mandatory inspection. Omar, in fluctuating crescendos, was whimpering with pain, and his answer to Sami's question was barely audible.

'Where's the box, Omar?'

'I'm… lying… on… it,' came the reply.

'Don't move,' instructed Sami. Little did he realise or care that movement for Omar was out of the question. Omar was convinced that not only was his back broken, but so were both his legs and one of his arms. He lay across the rear seat, head and back concealing the box, and at each bounce of the vehicle, as it responded to another obstruction, waves of pain engulfed him. The smell within the confined space was overpowering, and both he and Sami were covered with crawling flies. Sami mused that this could be to their benefit. He kept all the windows closed.

Sami approached the main gate with trepidation. The CCTV cameras were recording their activities and the central monitoring unit would watch it. Anything untoward would arouse immediate suspicion, resulting in a detailed search of the Mercedes. A security guard stood, blocking their path, his back to the main gate. A second guard appeared. He paused in the open doorway of the Security Office, as he surveyed the battered vehicle. Omar's erratic movements had slowed, with the consequence that the rear-end gyrations of the car were reduced to a slight, hardly discernable wobble. The second guard strolled towards the stationary vehicle, indicating as he did so that Sami should get out. Sami feigned confusion, pointing towards the back seat. He intended to keep the windows closed until the last possible moment. The smell within the vehicle was now overpowering and flies were everywhere. Omar's groaning provided a hellish background symphony, out of sync with the unremitting drone of insect noises. Sami watched as the second guard drew near. His timing had to be perfect. At the same instant that the guard bent to peer through the driver's side window, Sami slid it down.

The man recoiled in the blast of pungent super-heated air. The flies, bored with familiar surroundings, buzzed with glee at the new opportunity presented to them. A steady stream exited the open window and targeted the spluttering guard in their unending quest for new tasty morsels of food. As single-cell brains registered disappointment, they returned to the feast provided by Omar.

The guard, violently agitated, shouted at nobody in particular 'Shu hada? – What is this?' Directing his wrath at Sami, he shouted, 'IftaHel bab, ta'a la hone!' – Open the door, you. Come here!'

Sami, without moving replied, 'Please, I have an injured man in the back seat. I must take him to hospital immediately. I think he has internal bleeding.'

'Shu sar?' – What happened? demanded the guard in a commanding voice.

Sami explained that they had been inspecting Building 121. Omar had gained access to the upper floors. He had tripped in the dark and fallen through a hole, landing heavily on the ground floor. He was in a lot of pain and Sami was very concerned about his injuries. He must go to hospital immediately.'

The man wrinkled his nose as he approached and looked through the open window. He saw Omar lying in a haphazard heap on the back seat, twitching every now and then. Glaring at Sami, he returned to the office and made his mandatory telephone call. Within a few minutes, the main gates slowly opened and Sami was waved through.

Sami was elated. He had gotten away with it. Reacting to the adrenalin coursing through his veins, Sami started to sing; something he hadn't done for many years, much to the relief of his family. The old Mercedes rocked from side to side as it careered through the mid-morning traffic, Sami's sole thought being the sanctity of his office where he could gloat over the contents of his find in total privacy. Turning left into Rue Hamra, whilst ignoring the red traffic lights, much to the peril of those vehicles with right of way, he proceeded to turn right into Rue de Place, finally halting immediately outside his villa. Leaping out of the car, he flung open the rear passenger door, shoved Omar out of the way and, cradling the box in both arms, rushed up the path to pound energetically on the front door.

His terrified maid, sullen and browbeaten, stood trembling as he squeezed past through the widening gap and into the interior of the family home. Crossing the hall he entered the study and, with gasping breath, laid the box on the debris-festooned desktop.

The exertion had exhausted him. His face was ashen and he was breathing heavily. He paused, resting his bulk against the wall. Gradually, colour returned and with it, strength. Levering himself away from his resting place, he went in search of the maid, demanded coffee, and then sought out his toolbox. Returning to the study, he found awaiting him a cup of bittersweet thick black Arabic coffee. He purloined from the toolbox a metal bar and a couple of wrenches. Seated at his study chair he sipped the coffee as he examined the box. Opening it was quite simple. All that was necessary was to lever the staple secured to the hasp by the padlock away from the timber casing to which it was secured. Inserting the bar into the semicircular projection and using a metal spanner as a pad, he was gratified to hear the sound of splintering wood. The hasp was now hanging loose; there was no longer any problem in opening the box. Savouring the moment, he drained the last of the coffee and opened the lid. There, before him, lay a neat assortment of small hessian bags, each bound by a leather thong.

Omar had been conscious at the start of the journey. He had, early on, had the presence of mind to release the belt securing the box to his back. With each jolt of the vehicle he was unable to avoid the unwieldy box slamming into his unprotected head, and by the time they had reached the main gate, Omar was unconscious. He regained consciousness slowly. He gradually became aware that people were gathering around the open rear door of the vehicle. The sound of people penetrated his consciousness. He felt pressure on various parts of his body as gentle hands eased and guided his body out of its position, wedged as it was between the back of the front seats and the lip of the rear seat, his head hanging down into the foot well. He felt himself being settled onto a hard surface and water being forced into his mouth. He drank greedily. He opened his eyes and saw, staring down at him, an array of faces with, almost without exception, concern etched into their expressions.

'Are you all right?' one of the faces enquired. 'You look awful.'

'Do you want to go to hospital?' another asked.

A third voice, more distant than the other two said, 'Shall we summon a doctor?'

The refreshing liquid had brought Omar almost back to reality and he found himself propped up with his back against the side of Sami's parked Mercedes. He looked down with dismay at his pale spindly legs, protruding from soiled and torn underpants, his tattered shirt flapping around his bulbous belly in the morning breeze. Flies careered around him. His trousers, bereft of belt, had slipped off during his exit. They lay crumpled and discarded in the rear foot well inside the car. Humiliation surged through Omar's body at this shame. Tears welled up in his eyes and slowly rolled down his checks, hesitantly finding their way through ingrained grime and dust leaving, as they finished their journey, little clean pathways, as they dripped onto the pavement.

The onlookers retreated as if in rehearsed unison, to watch this grotesque figure as it wept, oblivious to the watching eyes. Gradually, self-pity was replaced by anger at his predicament. Levering himself into a standing position, Omar retrieved his trousers and slipped them on, securing them in place with his belt. Then, with purposeful steps, he strode forth to seek his tormentor.

Sami subconsciously heard the sound of the front door slam. He was too engrossed at the spilling contents of the hessian bags to pay too much attention to distractions. He had opened the first one, and to his delight saw a shimmer of gold. He had tipped the bag upside down and gold sovereigns had poured out, rolling and whirling around his desktop. Some had rolled onto the floor. Momentarily, he felt uneasy. Picking up a single coin, it felt light. He immediately saw, to his horror, that the coin was covered in gold foil. Peeling back the foil, he exposed a hard-boiled sweet. He picked up another hessian bag and emptied out its contents. The coins were the same. He was in the throes of emptying the sixth bag when Omar came storming into the study. Grabbing a china vase, Omar brought it hard down on Sami's bent head, shattering the vase in the process. Sami slumped onto his desk, head buried in the pile of little, round, gold coins. In his fury, Omar, snatched one of the hessian bags, shoved it into his pocket and rampaged out of the house, swearing as he did so that the relationship was at an end. The sound of the slamming front door rocked the house, but Sami didn't hear Omar's retreating footsteps.

Over the next couple of days, reports circulated throughout Beirut that Sami Hassan had suffered a nervous breakdown. His ringing telephone went unanswered and he refused to leave his study. It was rumoured that he was surrounded by a diminishing pile of gold coins and an increasing heap of gold foil. He refused all food and appeared to be sucking sweets. The strange noises emanating from behind the closed door gave every indication of an infestation of undisciplined flies.

Chapter 11

Six months have passed, and various Chancellors of the various universities in Lebanon, are reading their mail at different times, albeit on the same day. Their secretaries, charged with routing general correspondence direct to Heads of Departments, have sorted the opened letters into the various wire baskets, each labelled according to Department. University porters will at allotted times collect the mail for subsequent distribution.

At the American University of Beirut, the Chancellor's allocated basket contained lesser amounts of correspondence than his Heads of Department. Assad Khoury was a great believer in delegation. The morning mail contained the usual, but that day, jumbled in amongst the open letters was a large sealed white enveloped, addressed personally to Assaad Khoury, Chancellor, American University of Beirut, and marked 'Strictly Private and Confidential'. There were no distinguishing marks. The absence of any postage stamp indicated it had been hand delivered. Assaad, pince-nez perched on the end of his bulbous nose, regarded the envelope with suspicion. It was that time of the year when favours started to flow in. Asssad, a distinguished academic, had a low tolerance threshold with those influential families who sired offspring who, during their upbringing, were imbued with an attitude of complacency about their feeble contribution to society, and subsequently sought to compensate for these inadequacies by attending, at great cost to their parents, the prestigious universities. The endowments bestowed on the AUB had declined in recent years, partly due to the declining wealth of the country but more importantly to the attraction offered by the excellent educational facilities in Europe and America. To fill courses, the University had to balance the wealthy inadequate with the suitable poverty-stricken able. Much to Assaad's chagrin, the effect was to dilute the quality of education.

Assaad slit open the envelope. He extracted two pages, both closely typed and signed by an indecipherable signature. He started to read in full expectation of a 'favour'. The letter contained six paragraphs. He read the first three. Fearing that there was a mistake, he glanced at the recipient's name at the top of the letter. It was clearly addressed to him and the letter was dated three days previously. He read on and as he did so, his bushy eyebrows rose and fell in unison, like a couple of tiny white duvets, indecisive about covering the tired eyes below. He read the letter again and then for a third time.

The letter advised that a non profit-making trust had been lodged with the Bank of Beirut. The administrators of the Trust had been charged with the duty to acquaint the Chancellor that the Trust would pay those usual University fees for those students who, bereft of financial resources, demonstrated an ability to benefit from further education. The caveat to the letter stipulated that these selected students must serve their country in an approved capacity for a period of not less than five years. Interviews of candidates, nominated by the University, would be arranged with a panel of respected academics and educational psychologists. They would select and then monitor the progress of the selected individuals throughout the period of the endowment. The letter concluded stating the number of students eligible for consideration.

Assaad stared at it in disbelief. Other Chancellors had similar distraught emotions, albeit at different times of the day. Unknown to them, a similar letter had been hand delivered to a selected number of secondary schools throughout the country. Moribund school heads, weary in the pursuit of elusive parents, professing an inability to pay the annual school fees for their talented sons and daughters, bounced into classrooms and pronounced, to the accompaniment of rousing yelling and cheering, a school holiday for the following day.

★

Thomas Norman St John reclined in the Business Class seat next to Paul James on the MEA Flight direct from Beirut International

Airport to London Heathrow. It was Thomas's eighth visit to oversee the re-construction of the St George Hotel. He was well pleased with progress. According to his Project Manager's Report, completion would occur early next year. The quality of the work was impressive and he was impressed with the calibre of the contractor executing the works. There had been a bit of a tussle at selection stage. The Government had proposed a favoured contractor, but subsequent due diligence had shown that the company was partly owned by one of the Ministry officials, and its track record was poor. It had taken a meeting with the President of Lebanon to have this firm removed. Thomas's confidence in his own recommendations to appoint another reputable local contracting company had proved well founded. The project was proving an excellent example of talented teamwork, and to date had proved hassle-free.

His impressions of Lebanon, and what it had to offer, had veered over the months from tempered hostility to quiet confidence. He was impressed with the inherent talent of the Lebanese people. As if to consummate this developing appreciation, he had planned to take the opportunity to celebrate, with his wife, their 35th wedding anniversary in the bridal suite of the newly opened hotel. Thomas had already pencilled into his diary a date, six months hence. Thomas did not confide these future plans in Paul.

The two men chatted easily as the plane entered Turkish airspace about generalities, the project and the pleasure of working in Beirut.

Paul had joined Murhead International as Executive Business Director. He was extremely satisfied that the investment made by Murhead in the reconstruction of the St George Hotel was good and secure. Reading the minutes of the latest board meeting of the St George Hotel (Paul was executive director by virtue of Murhead's investment), he found glowing forecasts of future bookings. Old customers, delighted with the return of the St George's Club (as they called it) were placing bookings at a prodigious rate. New customers, influenced by their peers, were making enquires, and from the cultural mix, expectations had risen that the old magic, inspired by intrigue and secret rendezvous, was replicating itself to its former intensity. Wealthy old sheikhs, burdened with wives of superficial servitude, were booking whole floors as pieds-á-terre for their summer relaxation in the easy cosmopolitan environment and relatively mild summer heat. The hotel, once opened, could expect an immediate occupancy rate of 80%. The ballroom suite was booked for the next five years for weddings and conferences. It was unheard of in the industry. Paul was debating whether to indulge himself and whisk Caroline (his lovely wife) away for a surprise week's holiday in the Presidential Suite of the new St George Hotel next spring. Paul did not share his future plans with Thomas.

★

Since that eventful day some months previously, Sami had remained closeted in his study. Hardly stirring, other than to respond to the calls of nature, Sami's body, obese before, had become bloated. Transporting this bulk over even a short distance demanded enormous energy, evidenced by his rapid breathing and ashen appearance immediately after these exertions. It was cause for concern for his family and friends. The quantity of sweet wrappers was accumulating to such an extent that after each successive visit, the bathroom floor would have a light smattering, attesting to their adhesion to Sami's trouser legs. His passage between study to bathroom was clearly visible by the trail of golden coloured squares that marked the path of his shuffling gait. The housemaid regularly swept away the debris but within a couple of hours it would return. Initially, the debris had been light, but as the weeks passed, it thickened. It was only in the last couple of weeks that thinning was becoming discernable, evidence that the supply of new sticky wrappers was diminishing. Amongst the sticky litter, occasional black bloated flies could be seen, wings firmly stuck to the gold squares, and their legs waving feebly in the air as they prepared themselves for the great beyond.

Sami's wife had remonstrated with him on numerous occasions but his only response was to pop another hard-boiled sweet into his drooling mouth. His business interests had deteriorated. The telephone had ceased its endless ringing and now lay silent, buried under a gold-patterned carpet. Sami just sat and stared into nothing, his eyes unfocused. The villa, quiet before the event, took on a deadly hush, broken only occasionally by slight ripping sounds as buttons wrenched their umbilical threads from the mother fabric, soared in a prescribed arc and finally descended, where they mingled with the litter covering the floor. The eventual family conference could only reach the inevitable conclusion: Sami was committed to hospital, where, his doctors confidently predicted, he would spend the rest of his days.

Omar completed buttoning up his new suit. It was the second of the handmade suits that he had purchased and this was the final fitting. He eyed himself in the full-length mirror as his tailor fussed around, making adjustments. Rather portly, he thought as he compared his shape to a nearby life-size tailor's dummy. The cloth had been cleverly crafted to minimise Omar's distended belly. The lines falsified and flattered the rotund body inside. Omar's fortunes had changed. The sequence of events culminating in that awful episode with Sami were etched in his memory. He had hit Sami prior to storming out of Sami's villa, his emotions in turmoil, and it was only on his return to the family's tiny apartment that he had begun to contemplate the possible consequences of his actions. He fearfully expected draconian retribution. Hiding himself in the privacy of his tiny bathroom, he had untied the leather thong securing the contents of the hessian bag, which on impulse he had snatched from the stacked rows nestling in the ammunition box. The golden coins glistened in the afternoon sun streaming in through the grimy window. Released from their confinement, they poured into his cupped hand. The golden sovereigns chinked dully as they overflowed the chubby palm, cascading onto the badly worn tiled bathroom floor. Fearful days merged into terrifying nights as Omar waited for Sami's retribution. As the days and nights passed and nothing happened, Omar, through his bewildered family, made discreet enquires about his former employer. The rumours circulating gave Omar hope. As days became weeks and still there had been no threatening demands, Omar's confidence gradually returned. He began to relax, occasionally venturing out to old haunts, infrequently at first but increasingly as the weeks passed. His family regarded his absence from the apartment with relief. Omar had secreted the bullion in the water cistern of the only WC in the apartment and he would spent hours, closeted by himself, counting and recounting the gold coins, much to his family's discomfort. Obliging neighbours had provided alternative convenient facilities for the rest of the family. Uppermost in Omar's mind was his subsequent survival and his family's welfare. His income from Sami was at an end and he had lost his job down at the fish market. He suspected that the part-time position as waiter was still available, but it had no appeal. He needed a steady income for his family's sake. His confinement provided the opportunity to contemplate his future without any distraction. It was a couple of months before Omar summoned up courage to go and visit a distant cousin.

Abu Yassine was a trader. He had a small shop in fashionable Verdun Street. In amongst the modern fashion houses and delicatessens his little shop was an Aladdin's cave of treasures to the selective collector. He traded in antiques (some authentic, some of recent manufacture) and bric-a-brac of exotic nature. To swell his merchandise, genuine rubbish contrasted with the brilliance of the choice articles. In the dark recesses of the shop, away from prying eyes, Abu Yassine smiled with pleasure as he surveyed the piles of gold sovereigns set out on the tiny table. Omar sipped Arabic coffee whilst waiting for a reply, hesitantly made after concluding the lengthy preambles of their meeting. They had discussed the family welfare at length, the political situation and the business environment. It had taken half the morning for Omar to broach the subject of his visit. Eventually, Abu Yassine, aware of Omar's impatience, declared, 'Well, my dear cousin, I'm pleased that you have confided in me. Yes, these coins have a high value and it should be possible to dispose of them through my contacts. You must understand that the sale may take a couple of weeks.'

As is the custom amongst Lebanese families, trust is absolute, and it was with a relief that Omar left an hour later, leaving his fortune safe and secure with his cousin. The sale took three weeks and there was paid into a special bank account, in Omar's name, the sum of $60,000.00. Abu Yassine took 15%, but then, Omar reasoned, a favour given deserves a reciprocal one.

Abu Yassine also gave Omar other impeccable advice. Trusting in his cousin, Omar purchased the lease on a small shop in one of the shopping malls in the Beirut Central District. Foraging out into the various markets scattered throughout the country, he stocked it with local handmade merchandise. It was with considerable pride that Omar, standing beneath the large sign reading, 'Omar's Handicraft & $1 Shop', suddenly realised that he was a *proprietor*. Trade blossomed, particularly as the increasing numbers of tourists were drawn to the majesty of the developing Beirut Central District. The little shop, crammed with local wares, was a magnet for those wishing to possess a souvenir of Lebanon or as a take home gift for family and friends in other countries.

★

Ian listened attentively to the estate agent. They had viewed the property that morning and Janette had responded positively. They had taken the decision to move from Sevenoaks as, whilst the 'happenings' had diminished, the latest had created for Janette considerable embarrassment, and she felt unable to continue living in the area. The assault charges on Mr Portly had been dropped by the local Social Services offices thanks to Ian's persistency in maintaining that the incident was a storm in a tea-cup. Mr Portly's communicating skills were poor at best and Ian had threatened that should the office persist in their allegations, Ian would pursue a counterclaim of infringement of civil liberties. He had never heard of such nonsense. The matter was quietly shelved.

The latest incident could not be so easily shrugged off. It had occurred midweek. Ian had departed for London at his usual time and the boys had been packed off to school. Janette had planned a morning of housework, and that afternoon she was meeting her best friend Mabel at the Crumpet Restaurant for afternoon tea and a bit of a gossip. Afterwards she intended to buy a pair of rather nice lampshades she had seen earlier in the week in one of the local furniture shops. Janette was aware that her intimate circle of friends was shrinking for reasons she could not fathom out. It was about 10 a.m. when, during her dusting of the lounge, she happened to glance out of the window at the front garden. She stood petrified at what she saw. It was a typical suburban front garden: a rectangular lawn, herbaceous flowerbeds and a centrally located circular flowerbed. Standing stock still in the middle of the flowerbed was the grotesque figure of a totally naked elderly man. He stood stock still in the attitude of Cupid, the God of Love. Protruding from his flabby thighs was an enormous erect member covered, it appeared, in a gossamer-type of covering. Strapped to his back was a sandwich board and there, written in fluorescent yellow on a black background, Janette read: 'The Lord giveth her to me'. The man was staring at the house. Janette stood spellbound, afraid to move as the creature cupped his member in both hands and cried out, 'I'm waiting for you, my darling!'

Neighbours' curtains twitched and wobbled with excitement. Prying eyes drank in the obscene spectacle. It took some time for the police to arrive to escort the man back to the local sanatorium from which he had absconded the morning before. The police constable explained later that the elderly gentleman was quite harmless, although a public nuisance. The only article of clothing the man was wearing was an old condom. He had selected this as protection against the likelihood of rain.

Ian stated his terms for the purchase of the property with the estate agent, who conveyed these to his client. Six weeks later they had moved to a new neighbourhood, miles away from Sevenoaks. The fez came to.

The personal column in *The Times* announced the intended wedding of one Miss Samantha Louise Meakin to one Giles William Lawson. It did not convey the absolute happiness of the couple to the public reading the announcement. Felicity and John were delighted with the news. 'He's a grand chap, you know,' John constantly confided in his beloved wife. The wedding was planned to be held at St Mary's Church, West Horsley and John was already nervously rehearsing his wedding speech, much to Felicity's annoyance.

'Darling', Felicity pouted, 'It's six months yet. Aren't you being a bit premature?'

'Well yes, I suppose I am,' John retorted, 'but it's important that I'm word perfect, don't you think?'

'Of course it's important darling,' Felicity replied. 'But please don't talk for days, you'll send everybody to sleep'.

The same argument resurfaced at least once a week for the next five months. Samantha and Giles, deeply in love, were unaware of the passage of time.

Simon parked his Golf GTi 16V immediately outside the dry-cleaning shop on Clapham High Street. He had been fortunate to find the space in the crowded thoroughfare. Grabbing the soiled business suit, he was on the point of opening the driver's door when he saw, protruding from the inside breast pocket, a couple of white envelopes. Snatching these out, he casually threw them onto the adjacent passenger seat and emerged from the car. Having crossed the busy pedestrian flow, he entered the shop. The chiming of the shop doorbell announced his arrival and as if from nowhere a plump receptionist materialised. She greeted Simon with, 'Hello darling, what can we do for you?'

Simon explained that he only wanted the suit dry-cleaned.

'Okay then,' replied the receptionist who, sporting a small name badge crookedly pinned to her grey overalls, clearly went under the name of Sharon. 'Any special instructions darling?' Receiving a negative reply, she handed to Simon a docket in exchange for the grey, pinstripe three-piece suit that exhibited egg stains on one lapel. 'Should be ready by Thursday, love. Anything else you want?' Sharon's social life was going through a down at the moment, and this customer looked as if he could fill in a few empty nights.

'No thanks,' Simon replied. Exiting the shop, he retraced his steps to the parked vehicle. Sitting himself comfortably in the driver's seat he buckled his safety belt and, just before switching on the ignition, his eyes strayed to the envelopes.

One was addressed in his father's indecipherable script. Simon had long ago ceased to ponder how the post office could possibly make correct deliveries with that type of writing, but letters from father seemed to arrive at fairly regular intervals. He put it down to the fact that if it was postmarked Lebanon and contained a Lebanese stamp and the address was illegible, it was delivered to him. The other was addressed in bold, rounded handwriting and was from his current girlfriend, Jacqueline Wilde.

Simon had reached that divide in life when his contemporaries were celebrating either engagement parties or wedding celebrations. During the previous six months there had been a new announcement of matrimonial intent every weekend. Even Samantha had recently announced hers to Giles. Although this was fully expected, Simon was feeling a bit upset at the pending betrothal of his sister, notwithstanding that Giles was a great guy. There had been many drinking bouts with Giles, and Giles was clearly a man after his own heart. Simon's thoughts dwelt on his latest girlfriend, Jacqueline, and, as if to console himself in the slight feeling of loneliness that suddenly enveloped him, he reached over to the white envelope bearing her bold, rounded writing and extracted the folded letter inside. It was from his father. Simon thought that both letters must have arrived on the same day, and in haste he must have mismatched letters with envelopes. Out of interest, Simon started to read the almost illegible scrawl.

My dear Simon,

As you know the plan worked, thanks to your ingenuity. As a result we have established an educational trust to provide previously denied students additional facilities to continue their further education, where these students would benefit. Those qualifying must, after obtaining their degrees, contribute to the welfare of the country for a period of not less than five years. I know you know all that, as we discussed it at length, but I think it only proper that we fill you in on the missing details and finer points. It was a stroke of luck to find those hard-boiled mints wrapped in gold foil that so closely resembled the sovereigns in size! It was relatively easy to manufacture the hollow, tubular survey rods with screw tops.

Who would ever think of suspecting an innocent ranging rod! It was simple to smuggle the sweets onto the site concealed in the rods and relatively easy to switch the sweets with the gold bullion in the secure concealment of the old building. We had one worrying moment. The ranging rods, once filled with the sovereigns, were extremely heavy, but again luck was on our side. None of the guards had picked up any of the rods on arrival so they would not have noticed the change in weight on our departure. That is what we thought, but the rods were so heavy we had concern that the guards might become suspicious by our laboured walk. Mike Brady carried the majority of rods, whilst Mike Fleming and I had an easier burden, but we were sweating profusely when we reached the security guards. Fortunately, the guards suspected nothing and we were waved through.

We unloaded the coins in the security of a closed garage and stored them in a couple of buckets of waste engine oil. Thanks to your efforts we made contact with Sheikh Mohammed, the Saudi representative to the International Monetary Fund. As you are aware, he was very reluctant to help, but thanks to your intervention he cooperated and the bullion was smuggled out of Lebanon in diplomatic bags, and later deposited in the vaults of a reputable Swiss bank. Sheikh Mohammed kindly arranged, through the bank, the sale of the gold on the international market, and forestalling any awkward questions, arranged to deposit the proceeds in a special Trust Fund called the 'Lebanese Educational Trust'. You may be interested to note that the proceeds resulting from the sale was $2,280, 000, and it's earning interest at a rate of 5.2%. This is way above current commercial rates, thanks again to Sheikh Mohammed.

I must tell you that not all the gold was deposited. When I first discovered the bullion, I made a rapid bag count, and calculated the number of coins in a bag. On the final count, we were short by one bag! It may be that we either missed it, or that not all bags contained the same number of coins. Anyway, I digress. The Educational Trust has been established, and thanks to the law practice of Dr Abu Enien and with contributions from your practice, we have had no problems. The benefactor is registered as

'Anonymous', and we are delighted that both Dr Abu Enien and Sheikh Mohammed have consented to be controlling trustees.

Finally, and I feel I must tell you this, the two Mikes and I split one of the bag's coin count, three ways: Mike Brady, so he could take an extended family holiday to visit his beloved Nepal and to give help to some deserving causes; Mike Fleming to purchase a new Mini Moke with balloon tires. His old one really wasn't suitable for the aggressive traffic in Lebanon. He's had a few accidents and he's got to pay money to a few people. Apparently the new vehicle is being custom-made complete with bull bars and ejector seats. To make certain he's noticed, it's being painted a delicate pink with yellow flashes down both sides. I know it sounds ghastly but it's what Mike wants. Our portion is being reserved to give Samantha and Giles a special wedding gift. What about you, old boy? Isn't it about time you gave thought to the other side of life's coin. You can't go on partying forever, you know. I think that's about it for the time being, but thanks to you everybody is going to be very happy, by all accounts. We'll talk on the phone next week, telephone company permitting.

As always, your loving parents,

Mum and Dad.

Simon extracted the other letter from its mismatched envelope. He began to read the endearments written on the faintly perfumed notepaper, thoughts on a different plane, oblivious to the fact that he was being stalked by a hostile traffic warden, intent on fulfilling his quota for that day.